## 'I looked

Fiona was so [...]
that was very, very silly. [...]
you.'

'I'm glad you think so—although one worthy matron in that bus queue obviously suspected me of kerb-crawling.'

Fiona chuckled. 'What—in broad daylight?'

'Just what I thought, so if she reports me I shall call you in my defence,' Greg warned with a most engaging grin. . .

**Dear Reader**

March winds blow us good reading this month! Christine Adams' SMOOTH OPERATOR shows the useful as well as glamorous side of plastic surgery, while Drusilla Douglas has two sisters apparently after the same man in RIVALS FOR A SURGEON. Abigail Gordon's A DAUNTING DIVERSION is a touching story of a twin left alone to find a new path in life, and we welcome back Margaret Holt with AN INDISPENSABLE WOMAN. Enjoy!

*The Editor*

**Drusilla Douglas** qualified as a physiotherapist and worked happily in hospitals both north and south of the border until parental frailty obliged her to quit. When free to resume her career, she soon discovered that she had missed the boat promotion-wise. Having by then begun to dabble in romantic fiction, she worked part-time for a while at both her writing and physio, but these days considers herself as more the novelist.

**Recent titles by the same author:**

PARTNERS IN PRIDE
A DOUBLE DOSE
A BORDER PRACTICE

# RIVALS FOR A SURGEON

BY

## DRUSILLA DOUGLAS

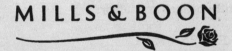

MILLS & BOON LIMITED
ETON HOUSE, 18–24 PARADISE ROAD
RICHMOND, SURREY, TW9 1SR

**DID YOU PURCHASE THIS BOOK WITHOUT A COVER?**

If you did, you should be aware it is **stolen property** as it was reported *unsold and destroyed* by a retailer. Neither the Author nor the publisher has received any payment for this book.

*All the characters in this book have no existence outside the imagination of the Author, and have no relation whatsoever to anyone bearing the same name or names. They are not even distantly inspired by any individual known or unknown to the Author, and all the incidents are pure invention.*

*All Rights Reserved. The text of this publication or any part thereof may not be reproduced or transmitted in any form or by any means, electronic or mechanical, including photocopying, recording, storage in an information retrieval system, or otherwise, without the written permission of the publisher.*

*This book is sold subject to the condition that it shall not, by way of trade or otherwise, be lent, resold, hired out or otherwise circulated without the prior consent of the publisher in any form of binding or cover other than that in which it is published and without a similar condition including this condition being imposed on the subsequent purchaser.*

*MILLS & BOON, the Rose Device and LOVE ON CALL are trademarks of the publisher.*

*First published in Great Britain 1995 by Mills & Boon Limited*

© Drusilla Douglas 1995

*Australian copyright 1995    Philippine copyright 1995 This edition 1995*

ISBN 0 263 78999 3

*Set in 10 on 11 pt Linotron Times 03-9503-57953*

*Typeset in Great Britain by Centracet, Cambridge Made and printed in Great Britain*

# CHAPTER ONE

FIONA GRAHAM actually had the back door open when her mother called out, carefully casual, 'Did I tell you that George Buchanan is back?'

Fiona gave it a second, wondering why this was thought to be the moment for such news. Then she returned just as casually, 'Oh, yes. . .'

'He's assistant manager now—and asked after you so nicely when I went in to cash a cheque.'

'That was kind of him,' Fiona answered woodenly.

'You may scoff, dear,' said her mother in a pained voice, 'but can you afford to be so choosy?'

Fiona lifted her big brown eyes heavenwards and prayed for patience. Never mind that she was progressing well in her career. She was an elderly twenty-seven, and six years working away from home in prime hunting grounds like Edinburgh and London, without a man to show for it, branded her a failure in her mother's eyes. 'Could we debate this some other time, please?' she called back. 'I really must go. It would never do to be late on my first day.'

That was the moment when her spoiled nineteen-year-old half-sister came into the kitchen, rubbing her eyes and demanding to know why nobody had told her the time. 'Hang on a bit, Fiona,' she commanded when she saw her sister backing out. 'I need a lift.'

'Then you should have got up a bit earlier,' Fiona returned crisply. 'I absolutely must go *now*.'

Deirdre's frustrated wail followed her across the cobbled yard to the garage, where it took five anxious minutes and several choice insults before Fiona could

5

rouse her ancient car and get it moving. Then she
headed north, away from Glasgow's prosperous and
leafy south side, towards the teeming, rundown streets
around the City Hospital.

As always at this time, the traffic was very heavy, but
long waits at traffic lights gave Fiona time to reflect.
Deirdre really was a pain. Or was it their mother's
uncritical adoration of her youngest daughter that was
really the trouble? Fiona's stepfather had always toler-
ated her very well but, naturally, it was his own child
who was the apple of his eye. Mother, however, didn't
have that excuse for her blind partiality. Its effect on
Fiona had been repressive to say the least and as soon as
her school and college days were behind her she had
decided to make a life for herself away from Glasgow.
She didn't regret the career move that had now brought
her back, but three days at home, relegated to her
customary back seat, had been enough. All the same,
she appreciated their having asked her to stay until she
could find a suitable flat.

Turning left at the hospital gates—and so technically
with the right of way—Fiona made a dash for it, beating
a sparkling new VW Passat by a whisker. But her elation
turned to embarrassment when her clapped-out Mini
died right there in the gateway, forcing the driver
behind to slam on the brakes.

Fiona switched on again at once but, though the
engine clattered and shook, it failed to fire. Meanwhile,
the driver behind had got out and was hammering on
the window, inches from her right ear. 'You're causing a
hold-up,' he yelled unnecessarily.

Fiona wound down the window and looked at him, a
crisp retort dying on her lips as her candid brown eyes
locked on to quite the most unsettling pair of smoky-
blue ones she had ever seen. She had to swallow hard
before managing to point out, 'My car won't start.'

'I'm not surprised,' returned the man, giving it a pitying glance. 'It's obviously terminally ill. You'll need to get out and push.'

For answer, Fiona turned the ignition key once more, treading hard on the accelerator for good measure. 'That's right—flood it,' said the man satirically. 'Oh, do get out, you silly girl!'

It wasn't that command, but the siren of an approaching ambulance that decided her. She leapt out, almost winding him with the door in her haste. Then she jammed her shoulder against the door-frame and heaved with all her might.

The man encircled her waist with a powerful left arm and whirled her aside. 'It's a good idea to release the handbrake first,' he said, speaking as slowly and clearly as he would to a dull-witted Martian. Then he leaned in, released it himself and shoved the car to the side of the drive.

Fiona had to stand there, trembling with humiliation while the wretch swept past in his beautiful car, followed by a sizeable convoy, with the ambulance bringing up the rear. She was praying that none of those cars contained staff, but without much hope. If Glasgow City Hospital's grapevine was half as efficient as it had been in her student days, then the story of the new assistant superintendent physiotherapist's inept arrival would be all round the place by lunchtime. And she had been so determined to make a good impression!

Still, she did make it to Physio before the boss did and was waiting in his office, a picture of the utmost efficiency, in her crisp new uniform of white tunic and navy trousers.

'I can't apologise enough for not being here to welcome you,' said Hugh Ferguson over a firm hand-shake. 'The traffic is chronic today and, to crown it all, I was stuck in the next street for a good five minutes. I

thought the lights had failed, but the gate porter tells me
that some silly lass stalled her car right in the main
gateway, of all places.'

'Ah, er. . .,' responded Fiona, going very pink. 'I'm
afraid that silly lass was me. My car is an antique and
the drive up from London has all but finished it off.'

Her new boss was a lot nicer about it than That Man
had been. 'It could have happened to anybody,' he
insisted. And while exchanging his jacket for a white
coat he gave her a very amusing account of breaking
down on the Kingston bridge during the rush-hour.
Then, having put her at her ease, he outlined plans for
her initiation. 'We'll get the inevitable paperwork out of
the way first,' he began, 'and then I'd like you to spend
some time on every unit over the next few days. That
way, you'll not feel too strange if and when you have to
take over at a moment's notice.'

It made good sense and as the morning wore on Fiona
appreciated his forethought more and more. By lunchtime, she had visited the medical unit and Intensive
Care. Now she looked forward to an afternoon of
orthopaedics and paediatrics.

Or, as it turned out, the other way round. 'I'm sorry,
but I've got a ward round at two so, if you wouldn't
mind changing, half-three would suit much better,'
explained Ortho's senior physio, an earnest-looking
woman in her early forties.

'There's no problem from my point of view,' agreed
Moira Smith, her counterpart on Paediatrics. 'What
about you, Fiona?' She and Fiona had been at college
together and knew one another well.

Fiona said either way would do as far as she was
concerned. She did have one question, though, and she
put it to Moira as soon as they were out of earshot.
'How come a girl of Marion Brown's age and experience
didn't apply for the deputy boss's post, Moira?'

Moira smirked knowingly. 'She *says* it's because she never knows when she will have to give up work to look after her mother, but I think it's more to do with Greg Monteith.'

'Who is he and how does he come into it?' Fiona asked inevitably.

'He's the locum consultant whose round she was so determined you shouldn't join, of course.'

'Ah, now I understand. They work well together and he doesn't want to part with her,' nodded Fiona. No surgeon liked breaking up a good team.

'Be your age, Fiona,' begged Moira. 'She's got a crush on him.'

'Ah!' exclaimed Fiona with great feeling. Had she not just put an end to a similar unsatisfactory situation down in London? Except that in her case the interest had been mutual, but as Michael had a wife he wasn't keen to part with. . .

'Exactly,' said Moira. 'Well, here we are, then, and I'm starting with the cystics, so you can just pop on a gown over that nice new uniform and give me a hand. There's nothing like clearing a few gummed-up chests for cutting a new assistant super down to size!'

During years devoted mainly to perfecting her neurological and manipulative techniques, Fiona had forgotten how copious were the lung secretions of a child with cystic fibrosis. She'd also forgotten the angelic patience most of them developed. 'Och, it's not so bad, miss,' said the fourth child she treated. 'Ma wee cousin has the cerebral palsy, and that's worse, I'm thinking.'

Fiona had often met adults with less common sense acceptance of the inevitable and her eyes were suspiciously bright when she rejoined her friend. 'I don't know how you can bear to treat children day in and day out,' she said fervently.

Moira shrugged. 'I look at it this way. Somebody

must, so why not me? And they've taught me so much. Children have this wonderful gift for cutting out all the waffle and going straight to the point.' She paused. 'I've some babies with bronchiolitis to see now, but if you're not feeling strong enough. . .'

'If they can bear it, I can,' Fiona retorted stoutly. She watched intently as Moira took each baby in turn on her knee, to vibrate its tiny chest with her thumb and two fingers, thus dislodging the harmful secretions for removal by gentle suction. But she was glad that Moira didn't suggest that she take a turn. 'What next?' she asked as they left the tinies' ward.

Moira said that she had some outpatients coming, but now it was time for Fiona to go and join Marion. Fiona couldn't believe how the time had flown. She'd lost all sense of it during those absorbing hours.

She found Marion hovering uneasily in the main corridor of Orthopaedics. 'I can't possibly show you round now,' she said bluntly.

Fiona lifted a puzzled eyebrow. 'But you said——'

'I know, but the ward round is just about to start. Greg—Mr Monteith—was delayed.'

'No problem,' returned Fiona serenely. 'There's nothing like a ward round for revealing methods. I'm sure he'll not mind if I tag along.'

But clearly Marion would. She opened her mouth and then shut it again with a tiny shrug of resignation, before ushering Fiona into Sister's office, where the retinue was assembling.

Discovering that she and Sister Sue Robertson had been at school together was a bonus that Fiona couldn't have hoped for, but all the 'Well, I nevers' and 'Do you remembers' were soon cut short by a man remarking in amused tones from the doorway, 'If you wouldn't mind postponing all this nostalgia, Sue, I'd really like to get started.'

Fiona gave a little shiver, before turning reluctantly round to face the man who had confounded her so thoroughly that morning.

He hadn't recognised her back view. Now, confronted once more with the dizzy female with the big brown eyes, freckle-dusted nose and abundant natural blonde hair, he gasped audibly.

'So sorry, Greg,' Sue was apologising cheerfully. 'First, though, you must let me introduce my old friend Fiona Graham, who is Hugh Ferguson's new deputy.'

'Hugh's *deputy*, you say?' he repeated, as if he couldn't believe it.

Everybody else in the room looked curious, but Fiona was sure that she understood. So many to choose from and they had to pick you, he was thinking. Somehow, she had got to make up lost ground. 'I come highly recommended, Mr Monteith,' she offered, even managing a slight smile as well.

'That goes without saying,' he returned wryly.

Fiona felt sure she'd got that, too. Giving a person a good reference was sometimes resorted to in order to get rid of them! Her smile faded and her determined little chin went up. She gave him a cool, grave glance before turning to Sue. 'It's great to meet you again, Sister,' she said, 'but I mustn't take up any more of Mr Monteith's valuable time. So I'll be going,' she added awkwardly, hoping for a speedy exit.

She didn't make it. Greg Monteith was built like a rugby full back and he was filling the doorway. He folded his arms across his impressive chest and stared Fiona down. Then he said, 'I don't suppose you came up here in prime working time solely to renew an old friendship, Miss Graham, so if your main object was to see how we do things, why not come round with us?'

'Oh, I—I couldn't possibly,' she stuttered, quite forgetting her breezy comment to Marion not five minutes before. 'I was given to understand that your ward round would be over by now,' she added, to let him know that this re-crossing of paths was not her fault.

His amazing smoky-blue eyes glinted for a second, but with amusement or anger Fiona couldn't decide.

'And so it would have been—on a normal day,' he agreed, 'but this one has been plagued with delays from the outset.'

Fiona knew what he meant by that, too. She'd never met anybody quite so good at talking in code. 'I really don't think——' she began.

'Havers! Of course you're coming,' he decreed, swinging round and striding down the corridor, irritatingly confident of being obeyed.

Fiona shrugged helplessly and tacked on to the end of the procession. Two brief encounters, and already she could tell that standing up to this man was about as pointless as opening your umbrella in a gale. She wondered why Marion hadn't picked an easier target for her devotion. But, to be fair, that wasn't really so hard to understand. By now they were just inside the women's ward and Greg Monteith was listening with apparently rapt attention to Marion's rather long-winded account of a problem. He could be kind, then. And patient too—sometimes! And he couldn't have been less like the earnest, bespectacled individual conjured up by Fiona's lively imagination when Moira had mentioned Marion's crush.

At thirty-three or thereabouts, Greg Monteith was definitely quite something. His physique was splendid and his strong tanned features were arresting beneath an abundant thatch of dark hair. Add those eyes—not to mention the smile with which he was now charming their first patient. . .

Fiona came out of her dream to realise that the whole

team was looking at her expectantly. She must have been asked a question and she hadn't a clue what it was!

Sue Robertson came to the rescue. 'I expect that Miss Graham would like to see Mrs Beattie's X-rays before she decides,' she said, thrusting a bundle into Fiona's hands. 'He wants to know how you'd treat this back,' she whispered urgently.

'Thank you, Sister.' Fiona turned away from the little crowd to hold up the first film against the light from the window. She studied it very carefully. The lateral view next and then the oblique. On the face of it, the slight misalignments which she detected should respond well to manipulation, but, on turning to look at the patient, Fiona noticed the unusual position of her right foot. It suggested muscle weakness. That could be an old lesion, but with no obvious muscle wasting, then—

'Do you always take so long to decide on a course of action, Miss Graham?' asked the locum consultant.

Yet another dig about their encounter that morning, she supposed. With an effort, Fiona kept him waiting a few more seconds before saying firmly, 'I like to think I take as long as—as a situation requires, Mr Monteith.'

'Is that so?' he asked with the merest twitch at the corner of his humorous mouth. 'So what physiotherapy would you prescribe for this lady?'

'None—for the moment,' she answered courageously. Or had that been rash of her? 'At least——'

'You got it right, so don't spoil things with a proviso,' he warned. 'Just tell us why you wouldn't treat her.'

'I'm assuming that this is a recent injury. . .' Fiona began tentatively, getting a nod in answer. 'So I need to know more about any neurological involvement before deciding whether or not manipulation is appropriate.' Me and my big mouth! I'll bet they discussed all that while I was daydreaming.

'I don't recall mentioning any neurological involvement,' he said, to her intense relief.

'I—um—noticed the position of her right foot.'

'Well observed,' he applauded, before going into a low-voiced discussion with the other doctors.

Fiona breathed grateful thanks to Sue for her timely rescue and Sue whispered back to think nothing of it, before advising Fiona to keep her mind on the job and off the latest boyfriend.

Considering who it was Fiona had been thinking about, that had to be the laugh of the century, but she kept a straight face and promised to remember. By then, Greg was examining the next patient.

Despite his late start, he took his time going round. Clearly, not only his treatment of dizzy females was thorough! As they returned to the office, Fiona was nursing the distinct impression that care was of the highest order on this unit. Unfortunately, she wasn't quite so sure about Marion's contribution. She wasn't incompetent, just rather old-fashioned in her methods and not too skilful at identifying her priorities. This wouldn't do in a senior who occasionally had students as well as junior staff to supervise and guide. Fiona's brows drew together in a thoughtful frown as she considered how best to bring that to the boss's notice. She was learning the hard way how it felt to be no longer just one of the crowd.

'That is some frown you're wearing, Miss Graham,' observed the locum consultant as they traversed the corridor. 'Do you disapprove of what you've seen here?'

That flustered her, as it was no doubt meant to. 'Goodness, yes—I mean no.' But she did, didn't she? 'Of course there are always a few differences between hospitals and I—I look forward to having a chat with Marion,' she concluded, that being about the best way of telling the truth without making waves.

They had reached the office now and Sue was assuming that Fiona would join them for tea. Fiona said thanks, but no thanks; she ought to be getting back to Physio to report on her first day.

'You'll also be wanting to see about your car,' supposed Greg Monteith, with a truly wicked grin. Why could he not forget her foolishness that morning?

'No, I am not!' Fiona snapped frostily, colouring slightly as she remembered where she was. 'That is, I phoned the AA at lunchtime, Mr Monteith, so it should have been towed away by now.'

'Good,' he approved. 'It was definitely in the way where it was.'

Marion, made miserable by all his attention to the new girl, promptly latched on to that. 'I say, was it you who caused all that trouble at the main gate this morning?' she asked hopefully.

By now, the whole team was smirking but, having almost lost her temper a moment back, Fiona meant to stay cool now. 'I'm afraid it was, Marion,' she confirmed. 'My wretched car couldn't have chosen a worse time or place to breathe its last.'

'At least it didn't let you down on the long drive home,' Sue comforted her.

Greg Monteith looked astonished. 'You don't mean to say you've actually been driving that thing outwith the city?'

'Certainly. Only last Saturday it did close on five hundred miles without any trouble.' Apart from overheating twice, burning most of its oil and constantly slipping out of top gear, but at least it got me here! she added silently. 'Well, thanks for showing me round,' she said, backing away before he could ask any more awkward questions.

'You're a brave one, Miss Fiona Graham—I'll say

that for you,' he conceded before turning to Sue and asking, 'Did I hear you say something about tea, Sister?'

'Ready and waiting,' she confirmed, before promising to give Fiona a buzz next day.

Ten minutes later, Fiona was telling her new boss how well her first day had gone. 'Everyone I've met has been so helpful and encouraging, Mr Ferguson,' she added. How about that for an example of turning the other cheek?

'That's good to know—and I'm Hugh to all my staff, Fiona. I'm either respected or I'm not, and what they call me is not going to change that. How did you get on with Greg?'

'Mr Monteith?' Fiona asked suspiciously, wondering why he'd been singled out for comment. Surely he hadn't complained about the morning's hold-up? With a generosity she was proud of, Fiona said, 'He comes across as very conscientious and competent.'

'Oh, he's that all right,' agreed the boss. 'And Marion? What do you make of her?'

He knows, she realised with relief. 'Well. . .she's also very conscientious—and caring.'

'And you're very diplomatic,' approved Hugh with a wry smile. 'I've been trying and trying to get her to go on a refresher course, but she always makes her mother an excuse, so I'm hoping that the "sitting next to Nellie" approach will do instead. So next time she's one short on the unit, I'd like you to step in.'

Before Fiona could comment, he had torn a sheet off the telephone pad and handed it to her. 'This message came through for you earlier. Not exactly good news, I'm afraid.'

Fiona took the slip and read that her car's starter motor was burned out, the clutch had gone and both the engine and gearbox were very worn. The conclusion was that repairs would cost more than its value, so Greg's diagnosis had been spot-on. 'I suppose I'm lucky that it didn't pack up on some lonely moorland road,' she sighed, trying to look on the bright side.

'I admire your fortitude,' said Hugh. 'Now, by a stroke of good fortune, I had the manager of the local Vauxhall dealers for a patient a while back, and he's still feeling grateful. I'm sure he'd be delighted to fix you up with a good low-mileage car.'

Fiona said that that was a kind thought, but unfortunately there was no way she could buy a flat and a car at the same time. Hugh then agreed that she had a problem, before packing her off with the warning that it would take her at least an hour to get home by bus.

A bright spring morning had long since given way to Glasgow's own special brand of relentless and penetrating drizzle, and as the bus-stop at the main gate was about as far as it could be from the physio department, Fiona was wet through by the time she reached it. Even so, it was an embarrassment rather than a relief when, after a brief incurious glance at the bus queue in passing, Greg Monteith stopped his car and reversed back to ask if she would like a lift.

'Um, thank you, but we're probably not going the same way.'

He raised a derisive eyebrow. 'You don't know that and you're clearly half drowned, so I suggest you get in while we debate the point.'

That tone of command again! Before she knew what she was doing, Fiona was in the passenger seat and belting up.

As he seemed to be heading for the Great Western Road, she said quickly, 'Somewhere near the Byres Road junction would suit me fine, thank you, Mr Monteith. If that's all right with you. . .' Suit her fine? Had she gone mad? It was way past the turn-off for the south side. And in such weather, too!

'Have you lived long in that district?' he asked conversationally.

'Where? Er, no. I've only just come back to Glasgow,' she explained awkwardly.

'You're a Glaswegian, then,' he assumed.

'Mm, yes.' Fiona wondered why she'd suddenly lost her tongue, when she'd always prided herself on being able to talk confidently to anybody.

'It's nothing to be ashamed of,' he told her, quite misunderstanding her reticence. 'I'm practically one myself.'

'Imagine that,' she responded foolishly.

'You're still feeling embarrassed about this morning,' he assumed next. He was a great one for making assumptions. 'There's no need, you know. It could have happened to anybody. Why, your boss——'

'I know. He told me,' she interrupted, and was immediately sorry as he gave up talking for a bit.

'What will you do about it?' he asked abruptly some minutes later. 'Your car,' he added when she didn't immediately answer.

'Nothing. I'm afraid it's past anything,' she said sadly.

'I think you're very wise,' came next. Since when? 'And when you're shopping around I think you'll find the new Golf is well worth looking at.'

Fiona didn't doubt it. The trouble was, she'd be hard put to it to look at so much as a second-hand car when a roof over her head was top priority. 'I'll bear that in mind,' she said, noting with relief that they had almost reached the stopping-off place she'd specified. 'Any time now, please, Mr Monteith.'

'Nonsense! I'd not turn a dog out in this rain,' he said firmly. 'Where exactly do you live?'

'No, really! I have to go to the shops,' Fiona claimed in a panic.

'Well, if you insist. . .' He slipped the car deftly into a

kerbside slot vacated by a battered van. 'I live about a mile further on,' he volunteered, 'so I could pick you up here just after eight tomorrow morning. On the other side of the road, of course.'

Fiona very nearly blurted out that she lived in Giffnock before remembering that she'd let him assume something quite different. 'You're very kind,' she had to admit, 'but I couldn't possibly trouble you.'

This time, there was no mistaking the grin on his face as he said slyly, 'It'd be one way of ensuring that you didn't hold me up again.'

'No—really,' she repeated desperately. All else apart, she'd have to be up by six to be here by eight.

'OK, suit yourself,' he said, casting a glance over her damp and bedraggled figure. 'But you'd be wise to bring a raincoat tomorrow—just in case.'

'Yes, I'll do that—and thanks again for the lift. . .' Fiona was out on the pavement by then, cross, embarrassed and miserable all at the same time. This is the first time I've felt so inadequate since I struck out on my own, she realised as she watched him drive away.

When he was out of sight, she crossed the road to get a bus back to the city centre. She was miles off her homeward route and it was raining harder than ever now. But no bus came and eventually, made reckless by despair, Fiona launched herself at a passing taxi and scrambled thankfully in.

That extravagance left her with just enough in her purse to pay tomorrow's bus fare. What a day this has been, she reflected as she ran up the steps to the front door. My first day in my lovely new job and what have I achieved? I've ruined some good clothes, beggared myself, and made the worst possible impression on the dishiest man I've ever met. I should have stayed in London! 'Anybody home?' she called as she stepped into the hall.

Her mother came out of the front sitting-room quickly enough to show that she'd been on the look-out. 'You came home in a taxi,' she said reproachfully.

'Yes. The Mini died on me this morning and can't be repaired.'

'But a taxi, dear—so extravagant. Why did you not take the bus?'

True to form and not a word of sympathy about my car, thought Fiona forlornly. 'It was raining so hard, I was late and tired and soaking wet, Mother.'

'I see,' said Mrs Crawford, in the tone she always used when she had something more pressing on her mind than your troubles. 'Come into the sitting-room, please, Fiona. I want to talk to you.'

'I'm wet through to my bra, Mother.'

'That's all right, dear—you may sit down on that old chair.' She shut the door. 'It's about Deirdre.'

When is it not? wondered Fiona on an inward sigh. 'So what's the trouble this time?' she asked.

Her mother frowned in reproof. 'You were very short with her this morning, Fiona. And she was very hurt.'

'Surely you don't think I should have waited for her?' By now, Fiona was feeling rather hurt herself.

'No, dear—not when she'd cut it so fine, but you could have been more gentle when you know how sensitive she is. She's had so many disappointments lately, what with Joel sneaking off to that job in Southampton without a word, and then the principal telling her she'd be better to forget opera and settle for lieder and oratorio.'

Deirdre's tutors had been telling her something like that ever since she'd started at the Royal Scottish Academy of Music and Drama, but to no avail. Deirdre stubbornly went on seeing herself as the next Dame Kiri. Still, if the principal himself had told her. . . 'Yes, that must have been a blow,' Fiona agreed, 'but I can't say I'm sorry about Joel. I only met him the once—when I came home last year for cousin Laura's wedding—but he struck me as being—well, rather flash.' Too late, she remembered her mother saying how much she liked him. 'But Dee is very young and so attractive,' she rushed on. 'There'll be others.'

'As to that,' said Mrs Crawford, brightening up, 'she did meet a very nice man at a party recently, and he's taking her out again tonight. The age-difference is rather more than I'd have liked, but her father thinks that's no bad thing. He says an older man will settle her down a bit, and have more patience with her than a boy of her own age.'

'So how old is he, then, and what does he do?' Fiona was asking practically when Deirdre burst into the room, wearing Fiona's newest and most expensive dress—a lovely thing of clinging sea-green silk jersey.

'How do I look?' she demanded, twirling round exuberantly.

'Wonderful, my darling!' exclaimed their besotted mother, just as her half-sister thundered, 'Deirdre! Take that dress of *at once*!'

Deirdre stopped twirling and her eyes glistened with ever-ready tears. She might not have the voice for opera, but she certainly had the histrionic powers. 'Oh, Fee—don't be so mean. It's just perfect on me.'

It was, too, but that only made Fiona more determined. 'That is my best dress and I've only worn it once. *Take it off*!'

'Really, Fiona! I'm sure your sister will take the greatest care of it, won't you, my darling?' Mother interceded.

'Of course I will,' agreed Deirdre airily as wheels sounded on the gravel drive. She danced over to the window. 'Too late,' she announced triumphantly. 'There he is. Don't wait up!' She snatched up her jacket and rushed out of the room. A moment later, the front door slammed shut behind her.

Fiona crossed to the window for a last sight of her precious dress. She forgot all about it, though, when she saw that the man handing Deirdre into his sleek black VW was Greg Monteith.

# CHAPTER TWO

BEING now without a car, Fiona got up even earlier next morning, and the first thing she did was to creep into Deirdre's room and retrieve her dress. It lay on the floor in a crumpled heap, but appeared to be undamaged. Thankfully she returned it to her wardrobe, which she locked up. There was no telling what else Deirdre might decide to borrow.

After supper the night before, when Deirdre was out and Mr Crawford had gone to his study, Fiona had tried to find out from her mother exactly how far Deirdre's latest romance has progressed. It hadn't been a helpful conversation. Mrs Crawford had wittered on at length about how attractive Deirdre was to men—something Fiona already knew very well—and how smitten Greg was, which was easy enough to believe. But when it had come to concrete facts like length of acquaintance and frequency and nature of dates, Mrs Crawford had been vague. 'Anyway, why are you so interested?' she'd asked finally.

'She is my sister,' Fiona had returned without so much as the flicker of an eyelid. 'Naturally I'm interested.' She'd seen no need to reveal that she'd met Greg, when all she'd been told was his name and the fact that he was a doctor at one of the big hospitals, though for the moment Mother couldn't recall which one. She'd then gone on to praise Fiona for her sisterly concern and to say that the dearest wish of her heart was to see her daughters each other's dearest friend—something so unlikely that Fiona had promptly changed the subject.

She was going over it all again in thought, though, on

this tedious bus journey to work. It was as good as anything for preventing worry about her present parlous financial state.

'Neurology and Geriatrics this morning, Fiona,' said Hugh Ferguson when he came dashing into the office. It seemed he never walked anywhere. 'How does that strike you?'

'Fine. I'm getting a look at the principal units in record time.' She paused. 'Hugh, about my own clinical work. . .'

'I ken fine you're dying to get your hands on some patients,' he joked, 'so I'm letting you loose on some of my biggest headaches this afternoon, while I'm at a forward planning meeting. And I'm still working on a tactful way to get you involved on Ortho. If Marion were downright incompetent, instead of merely slow and over-cautious, it would be simple. As it is—' he broke off, sighing. 'The boss's job is not the sinecure some of the juniors seem to think, Fiona.'

'I'm learning that—and fast,' she agreed. 'And you can count on my support at all times.'

'I sensed that at your interview; it was one of my main reasons for choosing you. That and your impressive clinical record, of course.'

'It was a longer short list than usual,' Fiona recalled.

'Because on paper there was little to choose between you all,' he explained.

'I see. Well, I hope I thanked you properly for picking me.'

'Indeed you did—and most charmingly,' he assured her with a grin, just as the senior on Neurology poked his head round the office door to ask if her high and mightiness was ready to inspect his unit. 'You always were the cheeky one,' laughed Fiona, who remembered him as well as Moira from college days.

Nothing to worry about here, she realised later,

having watched the way he handled his patients, and listened to his lucid and detailed accounts of treatment. 'Are you not a bit pushed, though, with only one junior to help you?' she asked.

'Only this week, while the other one is away on her honeymoon,' he explained cheerfully. 'And sometimes we have a couple of final year students, too. We get by.'

It was the same on Geriatrics. Good seniors are the backbone of the set-up—just like good ward sisters, Fiona was thinking as she strolled thoughtfully back to Physiotherapy at lunchtime. She was so preoccupied that she all but walked into the man coming towards her. She checked just in time, inches from an expanse of starched white coat. 'I do beg your pardon,' she apologised gracefully, just as he said jokingly,

'So you're a traffic hazard on foot, as well as in a car.'

'Oh, it's you,' realised Fiona, unaccountably flustered. 'I'm sorry, Mr Monteith,' she added belatedly.

'No damage done,' he assured her.

Fiona wasn't so sure about that, when one glance from those disturbing eyes could set her pulses racing like this. She was as pathetic as Marion, and both of them were wasting their time when Deirdre had already walked off with the prize. Say something, you idiot, she told herself. 'Then perhaps I should be fitted with hazard warning lights,' she offered, which was pretty good in the circumstances.

'Perhaps you should,' he agreed, his glance fixed firmly on her glowing cheeks. 'I've been thinking,' he said, 'and the upshot is—I think I owe you an apology.'

'You do?' Fiona gazed up at him, wide-eyed.

'It's very kind of you not to agree with me,' he claimed. 'You see, much as I hate to admit it, I was intensely irritated at first, yesterday morning, because I really was in a tearing hurry. I soon cooled down though. That car of yours was bound to break down some time, and you couldn't be blamed for it happening where it did.'

He'd called her a silly girl, though, when she'd forgotten to release the handbrake.

He was still apologising. 'And it was too bad of me to keep reminding you later on. Please believe there was no malice intended. I was only teasing,' he emphasised, in case he hadn't got through.

'I believe you,' she assured him. 'And I should have realised.'

'It's good to get that out of the way,' he said, with a warm smile, going on to say that he'd looked for her that morning.

She didn't understand. 'I'll not be working on Orthopaedics, Mr Monteith.' At least, not until Hugh works out how. . .

'I know—I meant at the junction where I dropped you last night.'

She was so pleased, and in the circumstances that was very, very silly. 'That was very kind of you.'

'I'm glad you think so—although one worthy matron in that bus queue obviously suspected me of kerb-crawling.'

Fiona chuckled, her full lips parting to show her small white teeth. 'What—in broad daylight? During the morning rush-hour? The woman must be paranoid.'

'Just what I thought, so if she reports me I shall call you in my defence,' he warned, with a most engaging grin.

Fiona just had to smile back. 'I'll be glad to, Mr Monteith,' she was saying, when another man with consultant written all over him paused beside them to request a word. 'That is, if you're not too busy, Monteith,' he added curiously.

It had been a timely interruption. During that chat,

Fiona had quite forgotten that last night Greg Monteith had been wining and dining her young half-sister.

Back in Physio, she shared a sandwich with Hugh in his office, while he explained some of the administrative paperwork, which was as copious here as anywhere else, nowadays. Except that from now on a fair percentage of it would be landing in her lap. All part of the price for progressing up the career ladder.

The afternoon session began at one-thirty, and when Hugh had talked about headaches he hadn't been joking.

'Good afternoon, Mrs McCafferty,' said Fiona to a formidable lady who could easily have been Greg's bus-queue adversary of the morning. 'I'm Fiona Graham, and——'

'Whaur's th'other yin?' demanded the patient indignantly. Well, patients often got attached to their physio and resented change, didn't they?

'Mr Ferguson has had to go to a meeting, so I'll be treating you this afternoon.'

'I hope ye ken whit ye're daein', then.' Patients often hoped that, too, but not many of them actually said it.

'Don't worry, I've specialised in problems like yours, Mrs McCafferty.'

'Ye'll be guid at the massaging, then.' Clearly Mrs McCafferty was one of those who attributed near-magical powers to massage.

'It says here that you've been having progressive manipulation.'

'Aye—but I think I'll try the massage noo.'

'I'll have a better idea of the most appropriate treatment after I've assessed you,' said Fiona firmly, in an effort to take charge.

'Ye're thorough—I'll say that for ye,' conceded the patient when Fiona had tested her back movements, palpated for painful points and tested muscle power. 'Noo am I gettin' the massage?'

'I am going to manipulate your back,' said Fiona, even more firmly.

'I hope ye ken whit ye're daein',' repeated the patient, bringing their exchange full circle.

Fiona decided to let the results speak for themselves. 'Do you feel any easier now?' she asked afterwards.

'I'll let ye know,' was the guarded response.

At least she didn't tell me she was worse, reflected Fiona as she saw Mrs McCafferty out with a cheerful, 'See you on Friday', before calling in her next patient.

Miss Simpson was a bird-like wee body with a voice to match and a perpetual runny nose. Instinctively, Fiona pushed nearer a box of paper wipes as she read the notes.

'Thacks, dear,' acknowledged the patient, pocketing the lot. 'I've got this thing called a polyester up ma doze and I'm waitin' on an op. It's a gey great nuisance, especially if I'm makin' something like custard. D'you know. . .?'

When she had to stop to mop up again, Fiona got in with, 'But what about your shoulder, Miss Simpson?' It was the reason for her referral and down on the card as just about immovable after an untreated fracture-dislocation, which Miss Simpson hadn't thought worthy of medical attention.

'Och, it's fine—just a wee bittie stiff, but could you maybe hurry up the ornithologist?' Fiona stared, bemused. 'Ma eyes is bad as well, so I'm waitin' on him too,' expanded the patient, impatient with Fiona's obtuseness. 'Between him and yon TNT man, I'm in a right guid pickle.'

Fiona made a note to check on her appointments with both Opthalmology and Ear, Nose and Throat. 'I'll do whatever I can,' she promised, 'but my job is to loosen your shoulder as much as possible. Is it not an awful nuisance too?'

Miss Simpson admitted that it was, a bit, with a patience that Fiona had to admire. In her place, she felt sure she'd be climbing the walls. 'Right! Lie down on the couch, please, Miss Simpson.' Not too hopefully, she placed one hand under the stiff shoulder and gripped the flexed elbow with the other. 'Relax as much as you can now, and let me take over. . .' This is a job for life, she decided when ten minutes' work yielded only about ten degrees of movement in any direction.

Mrs Buchanan came in next. She had two severely crippling arthritic knees, but had refused replacements on the grounds that 'if the Lord meant us to have that sort of thing done, he'd send us into the world with a bag of spare parts'.

But it wasn't all doom and gloom. The young lad with the ruptured thigh muscles was a laugh a minute, cracking jokes all through his ice-packs and ultrasound session.

Likewise the teenager with the severed extensor tendons of the right thumb, which somebody had repaired so skilfully. Fiona glanced again at the referral card. Greg Monteith, of course. Who else? she was thinking as the cubicle curtains were swished aside to reveal the man himself. He had a packet of X-rays under one arm. 'May I interrupt, Miss Graham?' he asked, which was very nice of him. There were surgeons who believed the world should stop for them.

'Of course, Mr Monteith.'

A quick, bright smile for Fiona before he bent over the patient. 'Right, Jackie, bend that thumb for me. Now straighten it. Still not all that easy, is it? But better than when I saw you in clinic last week.' He straightened up, smiling down on Fiona again. 'I really came to show these films to Hugh,' he claimed, 'but they tell me he's away to a meeting, so if you wouldn't mind. . .'

'Not at all,' she said. 'I'd finished Jackie's treatment, as it happens.' She told the boy the same time next day, before reminding Greg that there was a viewing screen in the office.

Fiona wished she weren't so aware of him close behind her as she led the way. Was it self-consciousness that made me trip like that? she worried as her left toe caught the edge of the office door.

Greg put out a hand to steady her. 'Careful, Miss Graham, or you'll be needing some of your own medicine,' he warned.

Do that again and it'll be Valium I need, thought Fiona. Her elbow was tingling away like nobody's business at his touch. 'Minimally clumsy, that's me,' she claimed.

'Nonsense!' he returned bluntly. 'You carry yourself beautifully. Such a good example to your patients.'

Fiona turned aside to hide her expression of pleasure at the compliment. Then she switched on the viewing screen.

Greg put up a film showing lumbar spine, pelvis and both hips. Then he invited her comments.

'Mature male,' she said after a second or two. 'With second-degree osteo-arthritic changes in the left hip. There's an old fracture of the body of the left ilium, just below the iliac crest, so those OA changes in the hip could have been precipitated by trauma. . .'

'They could be and they were—well-observed. Now raise your sights a bit.'

Fiona tapped the film in the region of the fourth and fifth lumbar vertebrae. 'Does he have referred root pain?'

'He does.'

'And you think that the slight irregularities here might respond to manipulation. . .'

'Do you?'

'All right, I'll stick my neck out,' she sighed, eliciting one of his smiles. 'Yes, I think it probably would.'

'But you're not one hundred per cent certain.'

'In this case, no. I think that would be—arrogant.'

'And you don't care to be thought arrogant. That's good. Arrogance is not an attractive trait in a woman.'

'That—depends,' observed Fiona thoughtfully.

'On what?'

'If a woman is also beautiful—and alluring. . .' Like my dear little sister! she finished silently.

'She would need to be both, and then some, to get away with arrogance, but we seem to be getting side-tracked.'

Fiona took that for a rebuke and, watching her colour rise, he realised that. 'Could you possibly spare a moment to come along to Outpatients and have a word with this chap?' he asked gently.

'Yes—but first I must tell one of my colleagues where I'm going.'

'I'll wait for you,' he said courteously. 'You'll not be familiar with the geography of the place yet.'

'Oh, but——' In honesty, she'd almost told him that she remembered it well from her student days. 'I'll be as quick as I can,' she substituted, dashing off to find the receptionist. The outpatient department was only two blocks away from Physio, so she would have to be a moron to miss it, which made Greg's thoughtfulness even more exceptional.

Making a brief examination of the patient and hearing more of his history convinced Fiona that he was indeed a suitable case for manipulation. 'Do you wish Hugh to treat him, Mr Monteith, or will you trust him to me?'

she asked when the patient had received his appointment card, and left.

'Of course I'll trust you. Hugh says you're an expert.'

Yet earlier, he'd claimed to be looking for Hugh. . .

'I'll be happy to treat your patient,' she said truthfully.

He gave her such a smile that she went quite dizzy, before saying, 'In that case, he's probably as good as cured already.'

Fiona returned to Physio in a daze. Never before had she been so quickly and so strongly attracted to a man. And if I didn't know about him and Deirdre, I could almost imagine that he fancied me, she thought. But I *do* know—and that's as well. Now I'll not go making a fool of myself by imagining there's more than there is.

As Fiona walked through the door, the receptionist came out of her cubby-hole. 'Sister Robertson phoned down from Ortho a few minutes ago, Miss Graham. She wants you to ring her back.'

'Thanks, Sharon.' Fiona went into the office and dialled.

'Fiona? Great!' said Sue. 'Listen, if you're not doing anything vital in about an hour, you're quite likely to find a nice pot of Earl Grey brewing in my office.'

Around five, with any luck, Fiona would be ready for a cuppa and Ortho was only three minutes away. 'That sounds like an offer I can't refuse,' she laughed.

'I hope you don't think I pass all day in idle chat and tea-drinking,' said Sue later on when they settled in her office with the door shut. 'There's something I simply have to say to you and I couldn't yesterday, with everybody around.' She stopped, a frown spoiling her pretty, good-natured face. 'It's about Marion, Fiona. I hate the idea of discussing her with the surgeons or with Hugh, so when you turned up yesterday it was like the answer to a prayer. She's very industrious—never idle for a minute—but she doesn't always direct her efforts

to—to the best advantage. You think I'm being offi-
cious,' Sue wound up defensively.

'Not at all; you've confirmed my own impressions, so
you can stop worrying. Hugh's already aware of the
problem and is working on a tactful way of resolving it.'

Sue said that was a great relief, repeated that she'd
nothing against Marion personally—unless it was a
tendency to follow Greg around—and then asked Fiona
for her first impressions of the job.

That was easy. 'I'm rather confused,' said Fiona,
thinking mostly of Greg Monteith.

'And having your car pack up like that must be a real
bind. Where are you staying? At home?'

'For the moment, but it's an awful journey and I'll be
moving if I can find something nearer.' The distance was
a great excuse when pride wouldn't let her admit that
she didn't really fit in at home.

'They want you to stay, of course,' assumed Sue, 'but
a girl needs her own space.'

Fiona agreed and they were discussing the housing
problem when Greg walked into the office.

'You're discussing cars,' he assumed, perching on the
edge of Sue's desk and rattling the lid of the teapot.

'OK, I can take a hint,' she laughed, getting up to
take another cup from the cupboard. 'And you're
wrong, as it happens. We're trying to find Fiona somewhere to live.'

'But I thought——' he began.

'I'm only staying at home while I look around,' Fiona
jumped in before he could expand on yesterday's
misunderstanding.

He flashed a smile of thanks in Sue's direction as she
handed him his tea, and then his eyes were on Fiona
again. 'So what exactly are you looking for?' he asked.

'What I would really like is to find a flat for sale that's

near the hospital, and not too pricey, but I know that's too much to hope for,' she wound up sadly.

Greg helped himself to a biscuit and chewed thoughtfully for a minute before saying to Sue, 'What about that place of Jenny Clarke's, if she hasn't sold it already?'

'Why didn't I think of that?' she exclaimed. 'I'll give her a buzz right now.'

'Who?' began Fiona, and while Sue was phoning, Greg explained in a low voice that Jenny was a sister on Outpatients.

Then Sue said she'd made an appointment for Fiona to view that evening at eight. 'Jenny apologises for the time, but she's not off duty until half-seven.'

'You could be in luck,' Greg said then. 'It's a super little flat and only just round the corner.'

And how would you know? wondered Fiona, before saying, 'Thank you both for thinking of it, but why is Sister Clarke wanting to sell?'

'You can forget noisy neighbours; she's just got married and her new husband has a larger place,' Sue explained.

'Well, I can only say that her timing was splendid from my point of view,' Fiona said happily as she replaced her cup on the tray.

'You're not going?' protested Greg.

'I must. My boss will be out of his meeting by now and I have a few things to discuss with him.' The truth, but not all of it. Fiona had been feeling more and more unsettled by Greg's frank and steady scrutiny. It's a very good thing I know about him and Deirdre, she thought yet again as she hurried away.

Mrs Crawford was pleased when her elder daughter phoned to say she would not be home for supper. 'That is really fortunate, Fiona. Deirdre, John and I have been asked to one of his partners' for dinner tonight, and I'd quite forgotten to make something for you.'

That was pretty cool, even for Mother, and perhaps she realised it, because she followed on with, 'But there's plenty of cold meat and salad in the fridge if you're hungry when you get home, dear.'

'Thank you very much, Mother, that's very thoughtful of you,' Fiona answered woodenly.

Mrs Crawford missed the irony. 'I always try to do my best for my family,' she claimed before hanging up.

Being left now with two hours to kill before her appointment to view, Fiona put in some time reading a pile of pamphlets and memos from Admin, which Hugh had set aside for her. Then she went across the road for a meal at a wine bar he had also recommended. Having ordered spaghetti and a side-salad, Fiona selected a corner table, away from the crowd. She had finished both her meal and the *Herald* crossword, and was drinking coffee, when she heard Greg say, 'So we meet again.'

She waited a second or two before trusting herself to look at him and then remarked calmly, 'At least I'm not posing a traffic hazard this time.'

He sat down and watched her fold her newspaper and reach for her bag. Then he said, 'If you keep on running away every time we meet, I shall develop an acute inferiority complex.'

That, she reckoned, was only slightly more likely than the sky falling in. 'But I've finished my supper, Mr Monteith, and now I'm off to view that flat you so kindly told me about.'

He eyed her through narrowed eyes before glancing at the thin gold Rolex on his left wrist. 'You don't need half an hour for a five-minute walk,' he said. 'So have another coffee and keep me company for a bit.'

Fiona obediently sat down again, although she had decided to stick to her guns. Greg ordered another coffee from a passing waitress, who brought it immediately. Fiona had expected nothing else. 'Do you come here often, Mr Monteith?' she asked, cringing inwardly at such unoriginality.

'Almost always when I'm on call,' he told her. 'All too often I've gone home and cooked something, only to be summoned urgently the second it was on the table.' The intent look she'd found so disconcerting earlier was back. 'Are you always so formal, Fiona?' he asked. 'I'd thought all that Mr, Mrs, Ms stuff had gone by the board between colleagues.'

Then why did he always call Marion Miss Brown? 'Not where I've been working,' she claimed.

'And where was that?' he asked predictably.

'London.'

'That's very enlightening,' he said with the ghost of a grin. 'There can't be more than two or three hospitals in such a small place as London.'

It was no use; she couldn't keep up a stiff front in the face of his determined friendliness. 'I've just put in three years at St Crispin's,' she admitted with a smile. 'And before that I worked for three years at the Royal Infirmary of Edinburgh.' Which was probably as good as telling him straight how old she was.

'And are you planning your whole career in three-year cycles?' he wondered with interest.

'I hadn't thought of it—why?'

'Let's just say I like to find out as much as I can about new colleagues,' he returned.

Was that really all it was? Could be. He might only be a locum while the incumbent had a major operation, but she'd never yet worked with a consultant who didn't want to know exactly what experience she'd had. So Fiona gave him a condensed version of her CV. Then she drank her coffee and called for the bill.

'I'll take care of that,' he said casually, as though it were nothing.

'Thank you, but I can't let you do that,' she insisted.

'You're saving up for a new car,' he reminded her.

'But not at the expense of my colleagues—however generous.'

'A girl of fiercely independent spirit, are you?' he queried thoughtfully.

'Absolutely.' She handed some money to the waitress and told her to keep the change. Then she said politely, 'Thank you for your company, Mr Monteith, but it is time I went now.'

He stood up when she did, saying gravely, 'I have enjoyed our chat—Miss Graham.' But she was left with the impression that under the gravity he was reading her like a book. A notion that fitted in with the idea of attraction dawning between them.

Now don't get carried away, Fiona, she told herself crossly. You know you've never believed in all that stuff about eyes meeting across a crowded room and wham! Besides, what about Deirdre?

As they had assured her, Sister Clarke's little flat in Brewery Court was just around the corner, in a street of warehouses and business premises, long since abandoned by the commercial sector and now being revived as up-market city centre housing. Fiona rang the bell, and when the heavy outer door clicked open she scorned the lift and took the stairs, gaining a view from a half-landing of a landscaped central courtyard, providing private parking. What a find in the centre of Glasgow.

On the fourth floor, she pushed through the fire-doors into a wide, well-lit corridor. Number forty-four was conveniently near the lift.

Sister Clarke was friendly and very practical. 'I've already cleared out everything I need, so if you were interested in the furniture as well it could save us both some hassle.' Fiona agreed with that, her spirits soaring as she was shown a small but well-equipped kitchen, a luxuriously tiled bathroom with a separate shower, a surprisingly spacious bedroom lined with fitments and, lastly, the showpiece of the flat—its large living-room with a panoramic view of the city skyline. The furnishings were modern, but unobtrusive, and Fiona was already imagining her own pictures and ornaments in place. 'I love it,' she pronounced. 'And I only hope I can afford it.'

Jenny mentioned a figure that was just about possible, especially as there would be no travelling costs. Then she suggested that Fiona could move in and rent until the formalities were completed. They settled on this coming Saturday for moving and parted, both well pleased.

Jogging slowly home on the bus, Fiona was thoughtful. Two more evenings and two more breakfasts with the only family she had, but with whom she never really felt at home. Could that be why she'd never been much good at forming close relationships? That must have something to do with it. If your nearest and technically your dearest didn't prize you all that much, was it any wonder that you didn't expect outsiders to? Then of course they didn't, because of the tendency to take folk at their own valuation.

Take George Buchanan in her student years—always telling her how cool and detached she was. Then in Edinburgh there was Mark, who more than once had complained, 'You're so self-contained, Fiona.' And most recently, in London, there was Michael. Was it possible that he had taken up with her because he'd sensed that here was a girl who lacked the confidence and push to force him to choose between her and his wife? She was incapable of pressurising or forcing the pace in any relationship. Doing that took a degree of self-confidence that she just didn't have on a personal level.

# CHAPTER THREE

WHEN Fiona told her family that she'd found the ideal
flat and planned to move at the weekend, they all took
the news completely in character. Despite being the one
to tell Fiona she was welcome to stay until she found a
place of her own, Mother now decided to be hurt. 'I did
hope you'd stay on with us, dear,' she sighed theatrically. 'Deirdre does so need the steadying influence of
an older sister.'

'I thought her wonderful older boyfriend was supposed to provide that,' Fiona retorted briskly, to which
Mother replied that yes, of course he did, but in a
different way.

'It's been very nice having you here,' declared Fiona's
stepfather, with whom she'd exchanged barely two
dozen words all week. 'Still, your mother guessed you'd
soon get tired of that long bus journey. Don't forget to
come and see us sometimes.'

Fiona hid a wry smile as she promised to do that.

Deirdre said not to be surprised if she turned up
looking for a bed after a late night in town.

Nobody asked Fiona how she proposed to manage
her removal without a car.

What she did was to hire a van, which she collected
after an early breakfast on Saturday, returning home to
find everybody out. She fared better at the other end,
where a pleasant young couple delayed their shopping
trip to help her carry things from the car park to the lift.
And on the fourth floor another neighbour helped her
transport her belongings to her flat.

It was unexpectedly warm for early May and the place

felt stuffy and airless. Fiona went round opening windows and letting in the subdued roar of the Glasgow Saturday traffic, along with a welcome current of air. She was longing to unpack and settle in, but the van must be returned and provisions bought. At last, after a late sandwich lunch, she was able to start. She was deciding where to hang her one good water-colour when the phone rang. She couldn't remember where she'd seen it, but traced the sound to a wall-mounted instrument in the kitchen.

'Fiona?' croaked a distorted young voice before Fiona could say anything. 'I can't raise the second on call and I'm in A and E.'

'Why?' asked Fiona, puzzled.

'Somebody let a door swing back in my face. I've lost a tooth and broken my glasses.'

So the duty physio is now a patient herself, concluded Fiona, while struggling to fit a name and face to the voice. She had to give up. There were eighteen physios on the staff and she hadn't been there a week yet. 'What fiendish luck,' she sympathised. 'Stay right where you are and I'll be with you in ten minutes,' she directed before hanging up.

She flung on a light jacket over her T-shirt and jeans, found her handbag, locked up and buzzed for the lift, her mind teeming with questions such as why wasn't the second on call at the end of a phone, and how the blazes had the injured one known where to contact her.

The second question was answered when she ran into Jenny Clarke in Reception in A and E. After saying that she hoped the move had gone smoothly, Jenny explained, 'Your poor wee physio was so reluctant to contact Hugh that I gave her your new number. I hope you don't mind.'

'Of course not—you were quite right. So where have you got her, Jenny?'

'Fourth cubicle on the left. She's too shocked to work, I'm afraid.'

Fiona realised that the minute she swished back the curtain. And the poor child was looking such a mess, too. Her face was bruised and swollen and there was a nasty gash on her forehead, presumably made by the broken spectacles. 'You're quite a picture, Sally,' said Fiona after a quick glance at the girl's name-badge. 'Does it hurt too much to talk, or can you tell me what's still to be done?'

'No, I can talk. Three in cardiac surgery and four in Intensive Care, then. . .'

When Fiona had written it all down, she asked, 'Did anybody see the accident, Sally?'

'Yes—dozens.'

The main entrance hall, then—it had to be—but why had she been there, so far from the wards? 'And did you recognise anybody?' Fiona asked next.

'No, why?'

'Because witnesses can be crucial in determining blame. That's why there's a space for names on the hospital accident report form.'

'Oh, lord. . .' Sally's bruised face crumpled and she seemed about to burst into tears. 'B-but it didn't happen in the hospital. . .' A painful pause and then it all came tumbling out. Rather than go for lunch, Sally had hurtled down to Argyle Street for a spot of shopping. The accident had happened as she'd come out of a department store. 'And the boss'll kill me,' she moaned. 'He's dead against us leaving the hospital when we're on.'

'Which is something you'll not be doing again, I fancy,' said Fiona, but her tone was gentle. Poor Sally had learned that particular lesson the hard way. 'Have you been given the all-clear to go home?' Sally nodded.

'Right then, off you go and I'll carry on here. And you'd better take a taxi.'

'I can't. I live out in the country beyond Bearsden and I don't have enough money on me.'

I'm a fool, thought Fiona, taking a five-pound note out of her purse; I should make her wait for an ambulance. But she said, 'Take this—and straight home, mind. I'll be phoning later to check.'

'Oh, I will, Fiona—I promise. You've been wonderful. I didn't dare ring the boss. . .'

But Hugh would have to hear all about it, and from Sally herself if she wanted to avoid too much of a telling-off. Fiona would point that out to her when she rang that evening. Meanwhile there was a mystery to be solved. In Physio, she checked to see who was second on call, and dialled his number. Still no reply. Seems I've uncovered quite a hornets' nest, she thought grimly as she changed into uniform before stepping into the breech.

It was routine chest care for all the patients Sally had listed—a matter of secretions to be loosened and propelled up into the main airways, so that they could either be removed by suction or expelled by coughing, if the patient was up to that. Routine, but time-consumimg, especially when you added in a few cheery words for each patient, introducing herself to those staff she hadn't met yet and washing her hands thoroughly at least a dozen times.

Fiona was in the office of ICU, deciding with the duty anaesthetist which patients required another visit that evening, when she became aware of a boy in physio uniform, hovering nervously in the doorway. She finished her discussion without pause, but when the anaesthetist had gone she said gravely, 'You and Sally are a fine pair, Angus. Supposing you give me your version of events?'

He was, it seemed, a keen rugby player who had succumbed to temptation and flattery when asked to substitute in the first team. The second on call was almost never needed, and one of his flatmates had promised to stand by to take a message—just in case. When he'd got home to find an empty flat and a frantic Sally ringing for the nth time, he'd come straight round to report. 'I'm really sorry, Fi—Miss Graham. I never dreamed. . .' He coloured and went silent under her steady gaze.

'Accidents happen—to staff as well as patients,' she said quietly. 'And that, as well as sudden upsurges in caseloads, is why it's necessary to have a second on call.' She gave him the evening list, with a quick rundown on the patients in question. 'And with Sally injured I'm afraid you'll have to work tomorrow as well. Here's my number in case you need help. You can be sure of finding me in,' she added, and watched him flush again. It was all the reproof she intended to give. It was for Hugh to deal with the pair of them.

The intensive care unit was conveniently situated between operating theatres and surgical wards and a group of staff dressed in loose cotton theatre garments was in earnest conversation outside one operating unit as Fiona slipped quietly past. Greg Monteith's powerful figure was prominent among them, but she didn't think he'd noticed her. But when she reached ground level via the stairs, he was just stepping out of the lift. 'You think I'm lazy,' he said with an engaging lopsided grin.

'I'd never dare to be so presumptuous,' she protested.

'On second thoughts, I'm inclined to agree with you,' he owned, falling into step beside her. 'You're not at all the girl I thought you were when you beat me to the gate that morning.'

'So what sort of girl did you think I was?' She had to know.

'Oh, impulsive, confident, carefree. . .' He paused thoughtfully.

'All that—just because I got in your way?'

'Plus the knowledge and good sense you showed later, on the round. I liked that. So it was quite a surprise when you turned out to be so—so staid and proper.'

That was one way of describing her refusal to respond to his friendly overtures, after discovering that he was dating her sister!

'I have a—a position to keep up,' she reminded him, sounding even more proper.

'So you have, but why are you here, keeping it up on a Saturday? Surely Hugh's never put you on weekend duty so soon?'

'No—I'm not exactly on duty. Just a few loose ends. . .' She was reluctant to reveal the shortcomings of her colleagues, but he read her answer as a rebuff.

'Then please forgive me for delaying you when you have so much on your mind,' he said quietly. He held open the door for her to pass out into the early evening sunshine, before striding purposefully away in the opposite direction.

Fiona continued on her way to Physio. She'd have to be a lot more diffident than she was not to realise that Greg's interest in her went further than the usual curiosity about a new colleague. And, but for Deirdre, she would have been pleased. More than pleased— elated. So how much did Deirdre really count with him? She would give a lot to know, but how to find out now that she'd left home? She could ring up on some pretext or other and then, just before hanging up, she could ask her mother how Deirdre's latest romance was progressing. But would she be any the wiser? Fiona knew from experience that her mother's reply was just as likely to be tinged with her wishes and hopes as with mere facts.

Next time I run into him, I'll be a bit more friendly, she decided. Where's the harm in that?

But more than a week went by before they met again. Fiona saw Greg several times—parking his car, lunching in the canteen, crossing the central quadrangle with other earnest, white-coated figures—but never near enough for a smile and a word or two in passing. She found that rather depressing.

'Nice weekend, Fiona?' asked Hugh, breezing into the office on her second Monday morning at Glasgow City Hospital.

'Lovely, thanks,' she responded, although it had actually been a lonely one and rather boring.

'That's good,' he returned, 'because you're going to be very busy this week. Marion rang me last night to ask for time off to arrange extra help with her mother. Apparently she's wandering day and night now. Did you know she has Alzheimer's disease?'

'I'd heard that she was ailing, but I didn't know that. Oh, poor Marion!'

'Your sympathy is well-placed,' approved Hugh. 'It's the relatives who suffer most in these cases.'

'And I'm going to be busy because you want me to stand in for Marion in Ortho.'

'It's the chance we've been waiting for,' he said. 'And you've got two very good juniors on that unit, even if young Angus Black does prefer rugby to physio on a Saturday.'

'But he'll not be mixing them again,' returned Fiona confidently. A very chastened Angus had given her the gist of his interview with the boss the week before, and she had stored away a few of Hugh's more telling phrases for use in any like situation.

A quick scan of patients currently on treatment in the four orthopaedic wards suggested that Marion had given most of the interesting cases to her juniors, while keeping the routine, undemanding work for herself. Fine—as far as it went. Youngsters needed to be stimulated and stretched, provided they were also advised and guided. At risk of having to stay late that evening to get through Marion's list, Fiona spent the morning with the juniors.

'You've got quite a caseload, Pru,' she began tactfully, looking on as the girl wrestled with a very stiff knee. She noted the tell-tale scars. 'Has your patient had a joint replacement?' Pru confirmed that, so Fiona suggested the electronic joint exerciser for such patients. 'Then you'd have more time for those who really need hands-on manipulation.'

Pru looked uncomfortable. 'Marion doesn't like it. She says it's too easy to get the resistance wrong.'

'Not if you test joint range and muscle power carefully first and adjust the thing to suit. Give it a go, Pru. You'll be pleasantly surprised.'

Then it was the boy's turn. 'I've always found that co-contraction techniques are more effective than using pulleys for the initial loosening of a very stiff joint post-injury, Angus.'

'I agree—but Marion says you can overdo and irritate the joint.'

'Only if you're—rather too enthusiastic.' Or don't know your stuff! she added silently. 'I think it's worth trying, though. . .'

'I've not done that since I came to this unit,' he confessed. 'So if you wouldn't mind checking my technique. . .'

'It'd be a pleasure. And any time you need advice. . .'

It went on more or less like that all morning. Naturally Sister Sue Robertson was in and out of the wards too and eventually she said to Fiona, 'I've been watching you and I ken fine what you're about. Well done.'

'Wait and see what happens when I get going on my own quota before you hand out any bouquets,' Fiona advised, laughing.

'Can't wait,' was the answer. 'And please let me know when you're ready to tackle our Mrs MacGregor. I want to be a fly on the wall.'

Fiona looked her up in Marion's file; a seventy-year-old with a run-of-the-mill fractured upper extremity of femur, pinned and plated by the senior registrar four days previously. 'Sounds absolutely routine to me,' she concluded. 'So what's the catch?'

'You'll soon find out,' grinned Sue, flying off to supervise a new admission.

'Are you coming to the canteen, Fiona?' enquired Angus at that point.

'Not just yet. There are a few things I want to check first.'

'Then is it all right if we go?'

Fiona was astonished. 'Of course! What else would you be doing while the patients are having lunch?'

'Marion likes us to ask her permission first.'

Did she indeed? How archaic could you get? 'I'm not Marion,' she pointed out.

'You can say that again,' they invited in chorus.

Fiona had read Marion's own notes about her patients, but a browse through their case-notes and X-rays would provide a clearer picture. She had almost finished her researches—making a few notes of her own—when Greg Monteith came into the doctors' room. 'What are you doing here?' he asked, sounding more surprised than pleased.

'I'm standing in for Marion Brown this week, so I was gathering some facts about the patients I'll be treating,' Fiona answered defensively.

'Which you have a perfect right to do,' he agreed.

'But I'm surprised Marion didn't tell me she was going on holiday.'

'She's not. She's having domestic problems,' Fiona replied diplomatically, not knowing if Greg was aware of Mrs Brown's illness.

'The poor lass! I suppose that means her mother is deteriorating.'

'Yes.' Why am I talking to him like this? So stilted and formal? Why can't I be natural?

He took his cue from her. 'I hope you enjoy your time with us,' he returned coolly.

'Thank you, Mr Monteith. I'm sure I will.' He was dismissing her, so she moved towards the door.

'Have you got all the information you need?' he asked.

'Yes—thank you.' Fiona got herself out in the corridor feeling very dissatisfied with that exchange. She'd vowed to be more friendly next time they met, so what had gone wrong? He'd first surprised, then chilled her by his manner—and she hadn't had the bottle to override that.

Preoccupied with these thoughts, she almost cannoned into Sue as she turned a corner.

'Great!' said Sue. 'Now we can go to lunch together and you can protect me from that biochemist who's been pursuing me ever since the inter-unit skittles tournament.'

'Would you like me to pop into the gym *en route* and pick up an Indian club or two?' joked Fiona. Funny how I can be natural and easy with everybody except Greg Monteith. . .'On the other hand, we could avoid him by not going to the canteen.'

Sue looked indignant at that and said she had as much right to be there as he had, which was quite true. But she's not as logical as I am, reflected Fiona.

The canteen was crowded, with not an empty table in

sight. 'Quick! Those two radiographers are leaving,' noticed Fiona, just as a big man with kind, steady brown eyes stood up and courteously offered them seats at his table.

Sue accepted rather offhandedly, then casually introduced him and his companion as Ted and John. Well, well, well, said Fiona to herself, having filled in the gaps with discreet glances at their name-badges.

John found his crossword much more interesting than his newest acquaintance, leaving Fiona free to observe Sue's polished demonstration of how to encourage a man without seeming to do so. It was very instructive.

'I'm afraid I wasn't much help to you back there,' remarked Fiona, smiling inwardly, as the girls returned to Ortho after lunch.

'No, you weren't, were you? Did you like John, then?'

Is she inferring that I was too interested in him to play nanny? 'How do I know?' asked Fiona. 'I only saw the top of his head.' A pause for effect and then, 'I was actually lost in admiration at the way you coped with your—um—unwanted pursuer.'

'Well, one can't be rude, can one?' asked Sue.

'I'll remember that next time I'm chased by a nice man I've no time for,' promised Fiona.

Sue had the grace to flush slightly before changing the subject by asking, 'Is there a physio by the name of Crawford on the staff?'

'I believe so,' answered Fiona after a moment's thought. 'I've certainly seen the name on the weekend roster, but we haven't met, so he—or she—must be on holiday.'

'It's a she,' said Sue positively. 'Are you going to treat Mrs MacGregor now?'

'I am—you've aroused my curiosity—but first tell me why you're interested in the Crawford girl.'

'I'm not, it was Greg who was asking about her. Apparently he knows her sister.'

So Deirdre must have told him she had a sister who was a physiotherapist at the City. And naturally he had assumed her name was also Crawford. He's still seeing her, then, Fiona realised, with an unwelcome little pang. 'Big romance, is it?' she asked offhandedly.

'What?'

'Greg Monteith and our Crawford girl's sister.' I have to know, but why did I put it like that? Muddying the waters. . .

'You can never tell with Greg. In the two years I've known him he's had more girlfriends than I've had hot dinners.'

'That I can easily believe,' Fiona returned grimly as they entered Mrs MacGregor's ward.

It only took a second to realise why Sue had singled her out for mention. She was nobody's idea of a little old lady. She was in the day-room, puffing energetically at a cigarette. Her ashtray was overflowing and her white hair had a yellow fringe, and not from peroxide.

'No wonder you've got such a bad cough, Mrs MacGregor,' smiled Fiona. 'You must be a very rich lady to afford that lot.' She nodded to the packets spilling out of the patient's cardigan pockets.

'Ma family's awfu' guid tae me,' was the answer in a hoarse croak. ''Specially on a Friday, when the grand-daughters have been tae the post office for the allowance.'

Fiona suppressed a grin. 'How's your leg coming along?'

'Och, it's OK. I s'pose you're wantin' me to do a Hielan' fling.'

'I'd settle for a wee dander down the corridor.'

'Make it a dander to the nearest bar an' ye're on!'

Fiona thought the woman's repartee was wonderful

and strove to match it. 'In case you haven't noticed, it's raining, so we'll save that for another day.' She planted Mrs MacGregor's Zimmer firmly in front of her and held out a helping hand. 'Come on, now, you must be awful stiff from sitting. . .'

'I'm gey sorry for the puir mannie who ends up wi' you,' was Mrs MacGregor's final shaft before yielding to the inevitable.

The walk over, Fiona insisted on a chest treatment which dislodged a formidable amount of typical smoker's gunge. Then, having restored Mrs MacGregor to her chair and her incendiary comforts, she went systematically round that ward, 'breathing and coughing' the chesty ones again, coaxing, exercising and mobilising. Most of Marion's patients were elderly and most had fractures in and around the hip joint, a frequent misfortune in that age group.

There were exceptions, though—like Mavis Blair. Mavis had been riding pillion with her boyfriend and had sustained a nasty fracture of her right femoral shaft when the bike had gone out of control and hit a wall. Her boyfriend was in the men's ward. 'So you've been here nearly three weeks, then, Mavis,' said Fiona when she'd explained about standing in for Marion.

'Aye,' agreed Mavis, casting a despairing glance at her elderly, sleeping neighbours. 'And I'll not be dyin' of over-excitement, that's for sure. Could ye no' ask the doctors to put Jeemsie and me in a wee room, with just ourselves? We'd not be gettin' up to naughties—not tied up like this. Though, knowin' Jeemsie, it'd no' be for want o' trying',' she added proudly.

'He'd need to be a contortionist, then,' estimated Fiona. Just like Mavis, he was trussed up in a full-length Thomas leg splint, with all the usual paraphernalia of weights and pulleys.

Mavis snorted loudly, getting a hiss of disapproval

from one of her neighbours. 'She's not sleepin', ye ken,' growled Mavis. 'She'll be up like a flamin' jack-in-the-box the minute she hears the tea trolley.'

'Which will be any minute now, so we'd better get started. I expect Miss Brown has explained why it's necessary to do the exercises?'

'Aye. If ye dinnae exercise when ye're stuck in your bed, the blood slows down and ye get clots—and if they stick somewhere vital they can kill ye. Joints seize up an' all and ye could be left a cripple.'

Quite a good, if very colourful paraphrase of the usual warning. Mavis had obviously taken the message on board, and ran through the drill of exercising every joint not actually immobilised, plus the foot exercises and static muscle contractions for the injured limb, like an expert.

'That was excellent, Mavis,' praised Fiona. 'You're so good that I'll give you a heavier weight to lift with your good leg tomorrow.'

'Life!' sighed Mavis, rolling her street-wise eyes up to heaven. 'It's aye the same. Do somethin' well and do they praise ye? Naw! They just step up the pressure. Gi'e us another sausage, hen,' she said to the nurse who was dishing out the evening meal. 'I've jest used up aboot ten thousand calories.'

Fiona was still chuckling over Mavis's psychological insight when she went to tell Sue that she'd finally finished work for the day. Sue wasn't there, but Greg was. He was hanging on to the phone, waiting, and turned to see who had entered. He gave Fiona a look of surprise before saying cryptically, 'So you can, after all, then.'

Her eyes widened with surprise. 'Can do what, Mr Monteith?'

'Smile, Miss Graham. I'd quite decided that you didn't know how.'

'Now look——' she was saying, when his caller began to speak.

'Don't go,' he said quickly when she made to leave.

'I'll wait outside,' she answered, going out and shutting the door. She leaned against the wall and wondered what he wanted with her. Was he going to tease her again—or pile on more work? The call took so long that Fiona began to think he'd forgotten her, but eventually he opened the door and ushered her in. 'You're very discreet,' he told her, 'but you didn't need to do that.'

'For all I knew, that was a personal call,' she said grimly, thinking of her sister, who was notoriously garrulous on the phone.

He shut the door and leaned against it, arms folded and looking as if he didn't know what to make of her. In the end he said, 'OK—I apologise. I shouldn't have said it.'

Now it was Fiona's turn to look puzzled. 'Said what?'

'What I did about you not smiling.'

'Oh, that! But you're right. I don't smile all that much.' Not at you, anyway. Not since I found out you're dating my sister!

He put on a look of exaggerated relief. 'For this reprieve I thank you. After I said that, you looked so fierce, I felt sure you meant to report me for sexual harassment.'

That was so absurd that Fiona burst out laughing. 'Good grief—I'm not *that* twisted,' she insisted as soon as she could speak.

'You don't see a harmless bit of teasing as verbal assault?'

'Of course I don't!'

'That's good. Sorry to hammer the point, but I do like to know where I stand. It's not easy being male these days,' he complained. 'If you don't open doors and so on, you're a mannerless pig. If you do, you're not treating women as equals. A man simply doesn't know where he is.'

That produced more laughter; Fiona had yet to meet a man more sure of himself than Greg Monteith. 'I've absolutely no objection to a bit of good-natured banter,' she chuckled. 'And anyway, I usually manage to give as good as I get.' Though I can't seem to manage it with you. . .

'You're definitely not a feminist, then?'

'That rather depends on what you mean by that over-used word. I expect equal treatment in the market-place, but I'm not in favour of positive discrimination.'

'You're speaking in a strictly professional context,' he noticed.

'Aren't you?' she challenged.

He fingered his jaw thoughtfully. 'I suppose so.' Didn't he *know*? 'Anyway, it was a professional question I wanted to put to you. How clued up are you on sports injuries?'

'As much as any other physio, I hope. After all, they form a major part of outpatient work these days.'

'But is it a subject that interests you?' he persisted.

'Yes, very much. As it happens, I was involved in setting up a special clinic at St Crispin's.'

'That's splendid. At least——' He broke off. 'I'd better start at the beginning. At the last orthopaedic meeting, a consultant from Glasgow General Hospital brought up the subject. We were all able to quote steadily increasing figures and, misguidedly, I offered the somewhat unoriginal reflection that prevention is always better than cure, so——'

Fiona couldn't help interrupting to ask, 'Why on earth did you say "misguidedly"?'

'Because I then got landed with the job of planning a campaign to that end,' Greg told her ruefully.

'Surprise, surprise,' responded Fiona with a rueful

little grin of her own. 'That's more or less how I got landed with that clinic.'

'And your experience of that would be invaluable—if I can persuade you to help.'

'I'd have to clear it with my boss.'

'Of course, but if I know Hugh—and I should by this time—he'll be all in favour.'

'Uh-huh,' observed Fiona, wondering how she would handle increased co-operation on a personal level.

'But you're not,' he presumed, 'so please don't feel pressured.' He had stopped smiling and Fiona realised he was very disappointed.

'It's a—a very worthwhile project, so if my boss *does* agree. . .' She left it there.

'That's great!' exclaimed Greg, sounding and looking so enthusiastic again that Fiona felt quite elated herself. It was almost as though they were conversing simultaneously about two different things, the one acknowledged and the other silent, unadmitted, biding its time. . .

Sue came in at that point, restoring reality with her offer of tea. Fiona thanked her and refused, pleading a mountain of paperwork to be completed before she could call it a day.

'I'd have thought that the paperwork was Hugh's job,' remarked Greg, frowning.

'Not all of it. For instance, he's delegated the on-call rota to me and I promised to have next month's list up on the board by tomorrow.'

'So that they can all start swapping round the minute they see it,' sighed Sue out of her own experience.

'However did you guess?' Fiona asked lightly. She gave Greg a brief, non-committal smile as she promised to mention his plan to Hugh and then she was out of the room, thinking what a good thing it was that Sue had come in when she did. She'd been letting her overheated imagination run away with her again. And yet, and yet. . .

Her colleagues were all away home by the time Fiona reached Physio. She picked up the nearest phone and dialled the Crawfords' number. No reply. She tried again after drawing up the duty rota and a third time much later, from home, and after supper. She let it ring and ring before hanging up reluctantly. How much longer must she wait to find out if Greg and Deirdre were still an item?

# CHAPTER FOUR

WHEN you lived alone, the phone rarely rang unless you were in the bathroom or taking something out of the oven. And when Fiona's mother rang next morning, Fiona was in the shower. She swore, wiped her feet on the bathmat, draped herself in a towel and ran to answer it.

'I thought you must have gone out already!' exclaimed Mrs Crawford reprovingly before Fiona could say anything.

'I was in the shower, Mother.'

'So you've got a shower, then—that's nice, dear. I want you to do something for me.'

Fiona said she would if she could and her mother replied that that was lovely, and it wouldn't be any trouble. Then she rattled on, 'Such a lovely dress, but it needed taking in. The shop can't deliver before Friday and Deirdre wants to wear it tonight. Buchanan Street can't be more than two minutes from your hospital so I told them you'd pick it up at lunchtime.' Fiona uttered a protest which her mother ignored. 'Then, if you take a taxi to Daddy's office, he will bring it home.'

'Mother, *please* listen. That would take at least forty-five minutes and I only manage about half that for a lunch-break. Why can't Deirdre pick up her own dress?'

'She's not going into college today. She's feeling rather tired and wants to be fresh for her date.'

'With that wonderful doctor of hers?'

'That's right. I didn't realise you knew about him.'
Oh, come, Mother! You told me about him yourself!

57

Fiona thought. 'Are you sure you can't do this for us, Fiona?'

'Quite sure, Mother. There is no way I can leave the hospital in the middle of the day.'

'They work you too hard, dear—you shouldn't stand for it. What time do you finish, then?'

'Never before half-past five.' So it's no good suggesting I run Deirdre's errands after work, she added silently. 'Look, Mother, I have to go now or I'll be late. Sorry!'

Fiona hung up. She was fizzing. That was the first time her mother had contacted her since the move and she had only done so now because she wanted something for her precious Deirdre. But that wasn't the real reason for Fiona's irritation. That was due to finding out that Greg was still taking out her sister. 'He can damn well find somebody else to help him with his ruddy campaign,' she muttered as she went to dry off and get dressed.

She was still planning how to thwart him as she crossed the car park at the hospital and noticed Hugh getting out of his car. Now if she could get him on her side, then. . .'I think I should warn you that Greg Monteith wants me to help him with a project,' she said as soon as they'd exchanged morning greetings. 'But with staff holidays looming and Marion off, I don't think——'

'The sports injuries awareness campaign,' he interrupted. 'He's already mentioned it to me and I told him we'd be delighted to help. A physio must be involved. After all, they do most of the hard work resulting. So when are you starting?'

How about that for a blowback? thought Fiona wryly as she answered, 'Nothing was decided. I told him I had to speak to you first.'

'I wish all my staff were as thoughtful as you,' he said

as they parted outside his office. 'Anyway, you can tell Greg you have my blessing.'

'You don't think that Marion may feel slighted?' Fiona asked desperately. 'After all, she is the ortho-paedic physio.'

'Only on the wards, and most sports injuries are treated as outpatients. See you at lunch.' In he went and closed the door.

So much for the brilliant idea of getting the boss to veto her involvement. Instead he'd practically ordered her to get on with it! But then I never was any good at getting my own way, she mused resignedly as she went to change into uniform.

When Fiona walked into Sue's office soon after, Sue waved some referral cards under her nose. 'Just in case you haven't enough to do already,' she said cheerfully.

'Great!' exclaimed Fiona. 'I had this feeling that today was going to be special.' She took the cards and flipped through them. 'A shattered femoral shaft, a tib and fib, multiple fractures of pelvis—I don't like the sound of that—and a dislocated hip. What happened? A motorway pile-up?'

'No—just a novel ending to a stag night,' returned Sue. 'The prospective bride was having hysterics in the corridor when I came on at half-past seven this morning.'

'No wonder,' sympathised Fiona. 'She'll be worried sick about her man, as well as disappointed about the wedding—not to mention the honeymoon.'

'By the look of her, she's already had that—and not just yesterday either,' returned Sue wryly. 'Time being clearly of the essence, we'll need to arrange a quiet ceremony in a side-ward as soon as the groom is out of shock.'

'That'll make a change. So how did all this happen?' asked Fiona, referring to the cards again.

'The best man got carried away and forgot his promise to stay sober. Then he drove into a wall at speed right after leaving the pub.'

'So no other vehicle was involved,' assumed Fiona. 'And thank God nobody was killed. At least. . .'

'No, there were no fatalities *this* time,' Sue confirmed grimly. 'Do you suppose folk'll ever learn, Fiona?'

'Some do, but there will always be those who never grow up enough to relate cause and effect. Any changes among the old stagers?'

'No—all as they were. And a good thing, too,' said Sue, returning with a sigh to the hated paperwork on her desk.

As Angus and Pru had quite enough work already, Fiona decided to add the new patients to her own list. So as soon as she'd treated her chesty patients who always merited what Mrs MacGregor called 'a good clear-out' first thing, Fiona went to the doctors' room to consult the relevant case-notes and X-rays. That done, she added a few notes of her own to the information she'd been given. She and Greg met face to face in the doorway. 'The new patients,' they said simultaneously.

He took her elbow, steered her back inside and shut the door. She had tingled at his touch and that annoyed her. Especially as he needn't have touched her at all; a simple request for two minutes of her time would have been enough. With tightened lips, Fiona took out notebook and pen. 'I take it you have some instructions for me,' she said quietly.

'You've come over all fierce and withdrawn again,' noticed Greg with a sigh and an exaggerated look of sorrow.

'Then I must learn to control my expression better. I *thought* I was looking efficient.'

'That too,' he agreed. 'In fact, I've never seen anybody looking more so.'

'That is—very gratifying,' claimed Fiona, raising her notebook a little higher, Biro poised.

He held her gaze a moment longer with a baffled, questioning look before giving up and asking how much she already knew about the overnight admissions.

'Names, extent of injuries, immediate surgical treatment and circumstances of the accident,' she reeled off crisply. All I need to know, come to think of it, she thought.

He was already sorting X-rays. 'This femur of the bridegroom's is a mess. In the present climate of rapid through-put—rather than the best possible end result—I'd probably have got a gold star for cobbling it together with wire and sending him home, non-weight bearing. But I went for non-popularity and a good result. We manipulated the fracture under general anaesthetic and put him in a Thomas splint. He's young and he's healthy so, given time, it'll be as good as new.

'There'll also be a spell in hospital on traction for the dislocated hip. The fractured tibia and fibula has already been reduced and plastered, so he can go home as soon as he can manage crutches.'

'And the fractured pelvis?'

Greg made a wry face. 'His main problem is a ruptured bladder, but the urologists will be looking after that.'

'What a way for a party to end,' she commented.

'Yes—it's almost enough to turn one teetotal. Any questions?'

'No—thank you. It all sounds routine from my point of view.' And not really needing discussion at all. . .

'Good. But if you need further enlightenment, please don't hesitate to ask.'

'I won't, Mr Monteith.' Fiona shut her notebook in which she'd needed to write nothing, and moved to the door.

'Have you spoken to Hugh about the sports injury thing?' he asked quickly.

'Only briefly—in passing. We'll probably discuss it at lunchtime.' She still hadn't quite given up hope of getting some other physio to take on the project. 'Now if there's nothing else——'

'Any word of Marion?' he asked.

'Not as far as I know, but she's so conscientious, I'm sure she'll be back as soon as possible.'

'No doubt,' agreed Greg, clearly less than elated at the prospect.

'Oh, there you are, Greg,' said Sue, pushing open the door at that moment. 'Message from the SHO to say that they're all ready and waiting in Theatre to start the next case.'

'Splendid!' exclaimed Greg, just as though he hadn't been doing his darndest to keep Fiona chatting for the past five minutes. 'See you later.'

He could have been speaking to either or both of them. Sue thought she knew and when he was out of earshot she said, 'If I hadn't heard him telling the houseman that he had a heavy date tonight, I'd think he fancied you, Fiona.'

'Then what a good thing you did listen in,' Fiona retorted crisply. 'There's enough gossip in this place without adding to it!'

Sue looked self-conscious. 'You mean about me and Ted Armitage,' she assumed as they headed towards the wards.

'I could always contradict it any time I hear it—if you'd like me to,' offered Fiona.

'You're a pal,' was Sue's parting response, but she hadn't said, Yes, please.

Only two of the new patients were ready for Fiona's ministrations. She went first to see Mike Brewis—the man with the pelvic injuries.

'I know that uniform,' he said warily as she approached.

'Don't worry,' soothed Fiona. 'I'm not going to ask you to climb the walls, but there is quite a lot you can do lying down. Here, let me show you.' She then took him through a simple routine of free and assisted exercises for the undamaged bits and underlined the importance of deep breathing, despite his bruised and battered ribcage. 'Better than getting hypostatic pneumonia,' she ended. That wasn't likely in a man of twenty-nine, but it had been known and it was always better to be safe than sorry.

'My mate should have been getting married on Saturday,' he told her, nodding across the ward to the bridegroom's unconscious form.

'We've had bedside weddings before,' said Fiona, 'so I'm sure something can be arranged.'

'Just as well, when our Sheila's got a bun in the oven——' He broke off. 'Have I shocked you, hen?' he enquired solicitously.

'Not at all—and he's doing the right thing by her,' she added, in line with what she perceived as his conventional view.

'Just what I told him. Sheila's ma sister, by the way.' He shifted in the bed and winced with pain. 'I hope this ruddy accident hasnae done for me in that department,' he groaned. 'The wife'd never forgive me.'

'I shouldn't think so for a moment,' Fiona reassured him bracingly, 'but if you're worried you've only to ask one of the doctors.'

He said he would, and then asked how his mates were doing.

Fiona told him what she could and promised to keep him posted. Then she went to see the man with the dislocated hip.

'They tell me this'll be a long job,' he began.

'I'm afraid it will, Mr McCurdy.'

'Och, you needn't be—I'm not,' he returned. 'I'm unemployed, ye ken, so this'll put in the time till the economy picks up—the way they keep saying it is.'

'That's an interesting point of view,' said Fiona.

'Aye—and it's got to be better than hanging around doin' nothing.'

'You'll certainly not be idle in here,' said Fiona, seizing the chance to explain all about the maintenance class which Angus now took every morning. Then she passed his card to Angus before starting on Marion's patients.

Just as yesterday, she got a growl for a greeting from Mr Barrie. 'I told ye, I'll do your damn-fool physical jerks when I'm feelin' better.'

'Which you are not likely to be if you don't do my damn-fool exercises, Mr Barrie.'

'Ye're an awful wumman! Yon Marion used to leave us alone.'

Did she indeed? 'Well, I'm different, Mr Barrie. I nag and I nag until I get my way.' Well, I do at work anyway. . .'Come along now!' Fiona went through the patter about stiffening up and risking blood clots, just as she had the day before. 'Imagine how awful life would be if you ended up chair-shaped and couldn't get out to the pub or the betting shop——'

'Here! Who told you I was a drunk and a gambler?' he demanded furiously. 'How d'ye know I'm not a God-fearin' church-goer?'

'Well, if you couldn't get along to the church, then,' Fiona offered after apologising for her mistake. 'Which church is it you go to, Mr Barrie?'

'Ye're right about the nagging,' he sighed. 'OK, then—anything to be rid o' ye. . .'

'Will I be in here long?' he asked when Fiona had coaxed him to exercise his injured leg—he'd been operated on for a fractured neck of femur—and walked him the length of the corridor and back with a Zimmer.

'You can go home as soon as you can walk safely with sticks and can climb a flight of stairs. So the harder you work——'

'Aye, I get the message,' he interrupted bitterly. 'Will you be back later?'

'Certainly—if you're volunteering for extra duty,' laughed Fiona, thinking she might as well go to Mrs MacGregor now that she was all fired up—Mrs MacGregor and Mr Barrie being two of kind.

After that came a session with Mavis. The girl's cheerful company was just the thing to set Fiona up for several more elderly patients, all in varying stages of recovery from that old-age scourge of a broken hip. And after that it was lunchtime.

Fiona was no more successful in changing Hugh's mind over a sandwich lunch than she had been first thing that morning. Hugh was delighted to have his new deputy working closely with Greg on such a worthwhile project, and so to tell him the simple truth—that she didn't want to work with her sister's boyfriend because she rather fancied him herself—was out of the question. And as she couldn't think of any other objection that wouldn't make her sound work-shy, what was left but to make the best of it?

Having accepted that, she naturally wanted to find out how much or how little was required of her, but Greg had a clinic that afternoon and wasn't expected on the unit.

As well as treating the rest of Marion's patients, Fiona found time to help Angus walk a very unsteady patient with crutches, went another round with the cantankerous Mr Barrie and helped Pru to set up a knee class in the unit's little gym, which Sue had said was rarely used. Then she checked the new patients again.

By now, Fiona knew that the best man who had been driving was the chap with the tibial and fibular fractures. He would be getting home as soon as he was safe on crutches—how ironic that he had come off so much lighter than his passengers.

With supreme tact, Sue had put him in a side-ward, away from his friends. He was very subdued and Fiona didn't refer to the accident. 'When can I go home?' he asked the second time he'd managed the length of the corridor.

Fiona told him possibly the next day, if he could manage stairs, the surgeons were satisfied with his check X-ray and his plaster cast was giving no trouble.

The bridegroom, by contrast, was very, very cross. 'With a best friend like yon, who needs enemies?' he kept asking. Fiona felt he had a point, but knew she couldn't take sides.

She had tucked up her last patient and was leaving the ward when a nurse came to tell her that Mr Monteith wanted to speak to her on the office phone.

'I'd be very grateful if you would call into Outpatients when you've finished work,' he said.

'I've just finished, as it happens.'

'Smart girl,' he approved. 'I'll expect you in three minutes.'

Fiona took three and a half and found him looking at his watch when she walked into his consulting-room. 'You take shorter strides—I should have allowed for that,' he greeted her.

Was that a joke, or had he really been counting the seconds? 'I stopped to post a letter,' she said.

'Such honesty,' he said admiringly. 'I like that.' His eyes were backing up his approval and that was very unsettling. Fiona wished he'd get down to business.

'So what can I do for you, Mr Monteith?' she asked,

which wasn't quite as sensible as reminding him that he'd sent for her.

A sudden gleam, a quick twitch of the eyebrows told her that he was thinking that too. 'Try sitting down for a start,' he said. 'You're not on a charge and I'm not a sergeant major.'

Fiona sat, feet together and hands clasped on her knees.

Greg continued to stare at her. 'All you need is a hat and a handbag and you'd look just like a nervous patient,' he pronounced.

It was only a second before Fiona erupted into giggles. Who could have helped it? 'You're a clown,' she said as soon as she could, which wasn't at all the sort of thing which an assistant superintendent physio was supposed to say to a consultant—even a temporary one.

But he saw nothing wrong with it. 'We seem to be getting somewhere now,' he considered.

'Ah!' returned Fiona, brought down to earth once more on seeing that look in his eyes again. She turned her gaze to the desk, and the slim folder on the blotter. It had a picture of a hurdler on the cover. 'You've already begun the sports injuries campaign, I see.'

'Yes—and we should talk about that, I suppose.'

Wasn't that why he'd asked her to come? 'Hugh's quite agreeable to my helping, by the way.'

'I know—he told me so himself. Yesterday.' He watched her colour rise before opening the folder and becoming businesslike at last. 'Some years back, when fitness and workouts became the in thing—followed soon after by a significant increase in sports-related injuries—the Glasgow orthopods mounted a campaign to educate folk about the dangers of inappropriate exercise. The physios were involved too, of course, and some elected to specialise in sports medicine.'

He broke off to smile indulgently at Fiona. 'Of

course, you're too young to remember the beginnings. Anyway, since then the thing has snowballed and we think it's time for a refresher. The idea is to give talks at public leisure centres, as well as any private club that doesn't have a qualified physio on the strength.' He paused again. 'There could be difficulties. Some of the trainers, such as ex-service PT instructors, really know their stuff, but those who have no training could be— obstructive.'

Fiona nodded agreement. 'I had one such for a patient once. He'd taken a correspondence course and his view of anatomy and muscle action was bizarre to say the least.'

'I can imagine. So how do you stand up to heckling?'

'On my own subject, no problem.' She raised a smile. 'Of course, if they were to throw things——'

'Then we'll both run for it.' Greg grinned back. 'The first meeting is scheduled for Monday next at half-six. Is that all right with you?'

Evenings; naturally it would have to be and she should have realised it. 'Monday's fine,' she agreed, 'but that's rather early—unless it's near here, of course. You see, I've not managed to replace my car yet.'

'That's no problem, because you'll be coming with me. Yes, what is it?' he asked in a completely different tone when the houseman tapped on the door and looked in.

'Sorry, Greg, but I was wondering if you'd mind checking a patient for me in Casualty. I'd ask the reg, but he's tied up in the plaster-room.'

Greg sighed. 'I hope you don't mean that literally,' he said. 'All right—I'll come. Six in the car-park—but we're bound to see one another again before then,' he said to Fiona. 'And thanks for coming.'

'Not at all,' she told his retreating back.

In the physios' staffroom, Fiona found Sally frowning

over the evening duty list. Her cuts and bruises from that brush with a swing door had faded and her new glasses were much more becoming than those broken. 'Six on ICU, four in cardio-thoracic and all these unseasonal bronchitises,' she was muttering.

It sounded a tall order for one. 'Let me see that,' Fiona requested. Then she said, 'Look, I'll take the medicals. That should save you a lot of time wasted walking to and fro.'

'Oh, Fiona, you are wonderful. . .'

'No—just practical,' Fiona disclaimed. 'And this is only a one-off—it just so happens that I'm not going out tonight.'

'I hope you're remembering that you can't start them before seven,' warned Sally, something that Fiona had overlooked. She would go home first, then, to put on the washing machine and boil an egg. It was great to live just around the corner.

When Fiona returned to the hospital later, Greg's car was still in its usual place and when she went home again at half-past eight it was still there. He was going to be very late for his heavy date with Deirdre. Fiona got a lot of satisfaction from realising that.

They were bound to see each other again before Monday, Greg had said when he'd gone off with the houseman after their discussion. That had been optimistic. The next day, Wednesday, was main ops day and there was a very long list. Then Marion came back to work on Thursday, in time for the round.

Fiona thought that Marion was being over-conscientious, but Sue said Marion was terrified to leave Greg unchaperoned any longer. Either way, it meant that Fiona was off the orthopaedic unit and Hugh regretted that. It would have taken Fiona longer than three days

to reorganise the work, but he could hardly order
Marion to take leave which she apparently didn't need.

Friday found Fiona standing in for Moira on
Paediatrics, a unit about as far from Ortho as possible in
that hospital. And she was off duty both Saturday and
Sunday that week.

'All set for tonight?' Hugh asked on Monday as he
and Fiona shared a pot of tea after their last patient had
departed.

'I'm looking forward to it,' she claimed, with more
tact than truth. Deirdre had looked in for five minutes
on Saturday morning, apparently for the express purpose of eulogising about her boyfriend. He was a lamb,
and a dreamboat. He adored her and indulged her every
whim. When Fiona, duty-bound, had offered coffee,
Deirdre had screamed and asked how could she possibly
when she was meeting 'Lambikins' at half-past? She had
then whizzed round the flat, said it was better than she'd
expected and departed, leaving Fiona sunk in despond-
ency and deep disgust.

Lambikins indeed! Greg must be completely besotted
if he let her call him that. And even more besotted to
arrange assignations for mid-morning when he was on
call that weekend. And she had thought him one of the
most dedicated and conscientious doctors she had ever
met. It was frightening—the way that passion could so
undermine a man!

'If you say so,' said Hugh, rousing Fiona to the
present.

'Eh?'

'You *said* you were looking forward to this evening,
but I'd never have known it from your expression.'

'Ah—yes, well. . .it's a while since I delivered a
lecture. I—I think I may be getting stage fright.'

'Then why not look out that excellent article you

wrote for the *Journal* a year or two back? It's all there, as I remember, so you'd only have to read it out.'

Fiona said what a wonderful idea and that she'd act on it, if need be. She was grateful to him for taking her excuse at face value.

The day had been hot and sticky, and when Fiona went to the changing-room she found quite a queue for the shower. 'Sorry, girls,' she said, 'but I'm about to pull rank. I'm working tonight—not going out to enjoy myself.'

Several of them told her simultaneously what they thought of a girl who couldn't see an evening with Greg Monteith as enjoyment. Fiona didn't answer. They didn't know what she knew.

She'd decided not to dress up, because her audience would probably all be wearing sports gear. A thin spotted cream blouse with a simple gathered skirt of dark green cotton would suit both the occasion and the weather. A wide belt with a fancy buckle emphasised her tiny waist. She brushed her short fair hair until it shone and re-did her make-up as soon as she could get near a mirror.

When Fiona reached the car park, Greg was already there, talking to one of the general surgeons. She hung back, waiting until they'd finished their talk, but as though he sensed her nearness Greg swung round, a broad smile breaking over his face when he saw her. 'Must go now—we've got a lecture to deliver,' he told his colleague.

The man turned round too, saw Fiona and promptly wondered—aloud—why his lecture sessions never involved taking out a pretty girl. Greg told him that was his problem, then he introduced them.

'Graham, Graham,' repeated the man. 'You're not the daughter of Ian Graham, the pathologist, are you? You're very like him.'

Fiona said no, Ian Graham was her father's brother.

'Funny thing, genetics,' the man observed, something neither Greg nor Fiona could deny, and after another comment on Greg's good fortune the man went off to find his car.

'So yours is a medical family, then,' assumed Greg when he'd seen Fiona into the front passenger seat with rather more help than she needed.

She waited until he was in beside her before saying, 'Not really—my father was a schoolmaster.'

'Really? So is mine. But you said "was". Does that mean he's retired?'

'No—he's dead,' she replied awkwardly. She was very uncomfortable, foreseeing embarrassment all round when he found out that she was Deirdre's half-sister.

Greg mistook her discomfort for sorrow. 'Oh, my dear—I am so sorry! That was clumsy of me.'

His sincerity was real and rather touching. 'Not really. How were you to know? Besides, it was a long time ago.'

'But you still miss him,' he assumed. Fiona nodded silently. She scarcely remembered her father, though she did miss having him.

'The tie between father and daughter is very strong,' he went on. 'I'm a clumsy oaf, Fiona, and I'll not let you make excuses for me.'

Deirdre is right, she acknowledged silently. He *is* a lamb. Lucky, lucky Deirdre. . .'You're very kind,' she said quietly. 'Now please be kinder still and tell me exactly what you want me to say tonight. We never did get round to the details.'

'Neither we did,' he agreed, sounding relieved at the change of subject. 'Supposing I describe the causes and types of injury and the surgical treatment, leaving you to give them the lowdown on how muscles actually function, the hazards of indiscriminate exercise, and, of course, the physical treatment. Does that sound like a fair division of labour to you?'

'It certainly does—and just what I had in mind.'

'So we agree for once. How splendid.'

She felt like a touch the quick sideways glance that came with his words. He might be madly in love with her young sister, but he was definitely interested in her too. No doubt about it. Men were like that, though— able to juggle several women at once. All those apparently happily married men with their little bits on the side. . .

'You're looking serious again,' remarked Greg as they set off. 'Surely you're not nervous?'

Fiona seized the straw. 'Just a bit. I was only saying to Hugh this afternoon that it's a while since I did anything like this.'

'It's very unlikely that there'll be anybody there with half your knowledge, Fiona, so hang on to that.'

'I will—and I expect I'll manage. Unless, of course, they do start throwing things,' she added, as she had when they'd first discussed this.

'In which case, we'll both do a runner,' he said, recalling his answer.

They both began to laugh, sharing a quick glance. 'Something going on there, I'm thinking,' observed one gate porter to another as the VW paused briefly in the gateway, before turning into the early evening traffic.

The centre they were visiting was a brand-new local authority complex about twenty minutes south-west of the city centre. 'Not too encouraging,' whispered Greg to Fiona when they entered a large gymnasium to find an audience of fewer than twenty.

'Perhaps the rest are already injured,' Fiona whispered back.

'Or preparing the missiles,' he just had time to suggest, before a very well-muscled lady leapt up on to a makeshift platform to ask, Wasn't it just marvellous of Mr Graham and Mrs Monteith to come all this way to talk to them?

Perhaps half of those present removed their hands from their pockets to clap briefly.

'Now then. Who'd like to go first?' she asked brightly.

'I will,' said Greg. He strolled over to a plinth and perched on one corner, swinging a leg. He's gauged the mood just right, thought Fiona, hovering between admiration for him and dread of her turn, looming.

Greg abandoned his prepared format and began by asking if anybody present had already sustained a sports injury. Eventually, a youth at the back sheepishly admitted to tearing a knee cartilage at football. That qualified as far as it went, although there were any number of ways of damaging a cartilage.

In simple language, Greg outlined the ways of dealing with such an injury, from rest to partial or total removal of the cartilage, according to the degree of damage. Then, with a wicked grin, he invited 'Mrs Monteith' to describe the post-operative treatment.

When Fiona had painstakingly described quadriceps drill for the important knee extensor muscles, from static contractions on day one, through increasing weight resistance, right up to vigorous weight-bearing exercises for the whole leg, the boy said airily, 'Oh, I never got none o' that. I was living thirty miles from the hospital, so they just put me in a stookie and sent me home.'

While realising that she was chancing her arm, Fiona invited him up to the platform to be assessed. I've done for us both if his muscles are A1, she realised in panic.

They weren't. The wasting of the affected thigh was obvious the minute he dropped his jeans, and when she measured both thighs for comparison there was a good three inches of difference.

This gave Greg the chance to highlight the importance of planned rehabilitation after injury. Then they each went through an abridged version of their talks, being listened to in silence, though not with much interest. The only question came from a girl who wanted to know if you could get plastic surgery on the NHS for any scars, if you did injure yourself.

The well-developed lady then wound up the evening by thanking the team from 'our wonderful Royal Infirmary' so much for their interesting talk, adding that she for one would never feel quite the same about hospitals in future.

'Do you think we did any good at all in there?' asked Greg when they'd finally managed to stop laughing at that double-edged parting shot.

'Definitely. Sitting still has to be less harmful than squash or jogging,' retorted Fiona. 'Honestly, though, Greg!' She'd never called him Greg before. 'Some people. . .!'

'Don't deserve to be protected from themselves,' he finished for her. 'Thank the lord this place is not in our catchment area.'

'And what a waste of a perfectly lovely spring evening, too,' Fiona lamented.

'But it's not over yet,' he said. 'What do you say to restoring our confidence with a healthy Mediterranean meal and some decent *vino*?'

'Ah!' said Fiona.

'You don't like Italian,' he supposed.

But what she didn't like was the idea of having dinner with Deirdre's boyfriend. 'Supposing somebody saw us?' was the verbal expression for her doubt.

'Are you saying there's a by-law forbidding hospital staff from eating spaghetti in public?' he wondered absurdly. 'And to think I never heard of it.'

Fiona had to smile. 'Actually, I was thinking more of the gossip angle.'

'Oh, that! No problem—we'll keep well away from the old place. I know a very nice little trattoria in Giffnock.'

He had to mean the Trattoria Napoli, literally just around the corner from home! 'The last time I ate there I was ill for days,' claimed Fiona, regardless of the penalties for slander.

'Then I hope you reported the fact,' was his reaction. 'OK, then, we'll go to another place I know of down by the river. I've never heard of anybody being poisoned there.'

Fiona said she hadn't either, so that was where they went.

'All the same, I shouldn't be here,' she decided as they were shown to a table by a very friendly waiter who seemed to know Greg well and viewed Fiona with interest. I should have told him I had a date and then gone straight home, she thought. I'm playing with fire here, and, being me, I'll get burned as sure as eggs is eggs.

'Yes, thank you, I love veal and mushrooms,' she agreed in answer to Greg's question.

The food came quite quickly and was absolutely wonderful, though Fiona hardly tasted it—or anything else of that meal. 'You're very preoccupied,' Greg said finally over the coffee. 'And I don't like it. It's anything but flattering. What's the matter?'

'Um. . .do you think the next talk will go any better?'

'I haven't the slightest idea and at this moment I really don't care. I've been plying you with food and drink and racking my brains for unforgettable witticisms with which to dazzle you—and all the time you've been fretting about a few nerds with no more than half a dozen neurones apiece. It's absolutely galling.'

'I suppose it must be,' she returned feebly.

'And I suppose it's something that you realise it,' he said flatly.

Fiona decided it was time to make an effort. He didn't know that she knew his interest was divided and this delicious meal, which he had so kindly bought her, was probably costing an arm and a leg. 'I've loved the frood and the wine and—and it's because your wit *is* so dazzling that I haven't said very much. How could I possibly compete?'

He eyed her sideways as if he wasn't sure he'd heard aright. 'You're either a lot more sophisticated than I'd thought or you're drunk,' he decided at last.

'It would be strange if I didn't know how to—to behave when taken out, at my age, surely?' God knows what I mean by that, she thought. I should have kept off the Asti. It always does this to me. One minute I'm as sober as a judge and the next I'm babbling away like—like a. . .'Forgive me,' she said, leaning forward and almost knocking over her wine glass in her determination to clear things up. 'That sounded as though I thought I was—that this was a date, but I know it isn't really; just a very kind thank-you for helping you out. Is that better?'

'No,' he said positively. 'If I merely wanted to say thank you, I'd wait until the series was finished and then give you a book token.'

'Ah!' said Fiona.

'You have an irritating habit of saying "Ah!" when you can't think what to say next,' he told her.

'Ah,' she repeated. 'Well, if you're not saying thank you, may I ask what this is all about?'

'You ought to know what it's all about when a man takes a girl out for a slap-up meal—*at your age*.'

I do know *that*, thought Fiona. All too often, it means he expects to end up in her bed. 'Yes, it was a slap-up

meal,' she agreed with a beautiful smile. 'I enjoyed
every morsel. It'll be my treat next time, though. That's
only fair. And I'm not letting you go out of your way
now. I can easily get a bus from here.'

'And get mugged on the way? That *would* improve
my standing with your boss. You can forget the indepen-
dence bit, because I'm definitely taking you home. And,
just to clear up any misunderstanding, I am not the sort
who expects to make free with your person just because
he's paid for your dinner. Is that clear?'

'Perfectly clear, thank you,' she answered in a very
subdued tone.

They didn't say much on the homeward journey and
the tension between them was uncomfortable. It was a
very good thing it wasn't a long drive. Judging by his
expression Greg was thoroughly exasperated, while
Fiona was deeply miserable at the way she'd bungled a
potentially promising situation. Promising? Was she
mad? The man beside her could very well end up as her
brother-in-law! And with that in prospect she had better
try to repair some of the damage.

While unlocking the outer door of Brewery Court,
Fiona swallowed hard and said awkwardly, 'I—I know it
may not seem like it, but the truth is. . . I've really
enjoyed this evening.'

'Have you?' he asked, sounding astonished.

'Yes, I have. You're—very good company and you
make me laugh. You're so witty.'

'Now I'm more confused than ever,' said Greg. 'If
that is really true, then why do you keep on putting up
the shutters?'

She couldn't possibly tell him *that*! 'I came back to
Glasgow after ending a rather traumatic relationship
with a colleague,' she said after a moment's thought.
'And that has taught me not to mix business with

pleasure.' Very neat—and very plausible, as well as true.

'Was he married?' asked Greg, going straight to the point.

Fiona nodded, amazed at his perception.

'Well I'm not,' he said. 'Think about that, because it makes all the difference.' Then he bent down and kissed her full on the mouth. 'Think,' he whispered, before propelling her gently into the building and returning to his car.

# CHAPTER FIVE

FIONA slept through her alarm next morning. 'Think,' Greg had ordered, and that she had. The upshot was a decision to give Deirdre a run for her money, rather than simply handing Greg to her sister on the proverbial plate. The exciting possibilities that decision opened up had been enough to keep Fiona awake until the small hours. As a result she only got to work on time by showering at the speed of light and giving breakfast the go-by.

Once in uniform she went to look for Hugh, but couldn't find him. Puzzled, she sought out Sharon, the receptionist. 'Does Mr Ferguson have an early meeting today, or what?' she asked.

In reply the girl said accusingly, 'You're late.'

Fiona blinked. 'Two minutes at the most—not the hour *you* managed to be adrift the other day. Now, have you or have you not seen Mr Ferguson?'

'He's in the Western General.'

Not at—in. 'Surely you don't mean——?'

'Boys out joy-riding in a stolen car. They hit him sideways on and pushed him through a wall and down a bank. It's a miracle he didn't end up in the canal.'

'In his car?' Fiona asked dazedly.

'Of course in his car. Mrs Ferguson phoned asking to speak to you, but I had to tell her you weren't here yet.'

Fiona got herself together and administered a cool look of warning. 'So I am now in effect the boss, then,' she said pointedly. 'Thank you for letting me know.' She then went back to the office to check Hugh's diary for that day. Apart from the usual string of outpatients, he had a heads of department meeting at eleven and a class of first-year nursing students coming at three. Quite a quiet day by his standards, so it could have been worse. Then she found his home number and phoned his wife.

'Fractured ribs, a smashed-up femur and mild concussion,' recited Carol Ferguson in response to Fiona's anxious question. 'He says it could have been much worse, but to me that's quite enough. They had to— to. . .' She faltered, then went on, 'They had to cut him out of the car and they said—they said it was a miracle he wasn't killed!' Another pause and then Carol continued, 'He gave me a list of things for you—just a second and I'll read it out.' She reeled off a list of items to add to what was in the diary. Phew! There would be no time for Fiona to begin her Deirdre-elimination policy today. They talked a few minutes longer about Hugh's injuries, with Fiona doing her best to relieve Carol's anxiety. Carol taught history part-time, and freely admitted how hazy she was about things medical.

Fiona was wondering how to wind up this call without offending the boss's wife, when the senior on Outpatients came seeking her, thus providing the excuse Fiona needed.

The girls decided to split Hugh's list between them and the first patient to come Fiona's way was Miss Simpson with the frozen shoulder, whom she'd treated for Hugh in her early days at the hospital. 'What a difference!' she exclaimed on checking that lady's movements.

'Aye, but I'm still waitin' on ma eyes an' nose. And ma teeth's no what they should be neither.'

'All outside our province, I'm afraid,' Fiona returned thankfully.

'More's the pity. Yon Ferguson mannie's gey guid at fixing. And he doesnae hurt us, neither,' she reproved

when Fiona applied over-pressure at the extreme range
of elevation.

It was always difficult, taking over another physio's
patients, and so it went on. First there was the macho
steel erector who objected to 'a wumman' telling him
what to do and then the suave businessman who thought
it beneath his dignity to be treated by anybody but the
boss.

Fiona soon put them both in the picture. All the
same, it would have been easier had Hugh been one of
those bosses who went to ground under all the paperwork, instead of compressing it to a minimum and
taking on such a heavy caseload.

'I have been waiting nearly twenty minutes, Miss
Graham,' complained one of Fiona's own patients
plaintively.

'Just five minutes more, Mrs Rintoul, but with Mr
Ferguson a patient in hospital himself we're a bit pushed
this morning. But you could go and get ready in cubicle
nine. . .'

Fortunately one of Hugh's instructions, relayed by
Carol, was to forget about the heads of department
meeting and just send his apologies, so by working
through the lunch-hour they gradually caught up.

They got behind again in the afternoon, though, when
Fiona had to break off to speak to the student nurses. It
was vital to give students in any discipline some insight
into the work done by all the other hands-on profes-
sions, as there was so much overlap, both in care and
observation. Fiona reeled off the main physiotherapy
techniques and their application in the most common
complaints and finally raised a laugh by saying that
student physios were also taught such basic nursing
skills as bed-making and the giving out of bedpans, and
were expected to leave their patients tidy and comfortable at the end of treatment. Then she demonstrated

some lifting techniques for helpless patients, which placed the minimum of strain on the lifters. 'We're all in this together,' she wound up. 'We need you, you need us, and the patients need us all.'

'You didn't mention doctors,' remembered a chubby-cheeked seventeen-year-old.

Fiona said that doctors certainly had their uses, but she'd leave them to put their own case.

'You struck just the right note all through, Miss Graham,' congratulated the lecturer who had come with the class.

'You took far longer than the boss does,' rebuked the receptionist when the students had gone.

Fiona eyed her calmly before asking quietly, 'Have you made those phone calls I mentioned yet?'

'Um, no—I've been too busy.'

Fiona then wondered aloud if Sharon might not have found the time had she not felt obliged to oversee her own activities. Then, hoping that she'd sorted out that problem, she went to catch up on the patients.

'How do you like being in charge?' asked Moira from Paediatrics as they were getting out of uniform at the end of the day.

'I don't,' Fiona returned bluntly. 'Especially when I'm constantly compared unfavourably with Hugh.'

'Young Sharon,' guessed Moira. 'Take no notice! She's got a crush on him, that's all.'

'According to you, the place is full of folk with crushes,' laughed Fiona.

'So it is—and not all the sufferers are females either. How did last night's talk go?'

Fiona got the implication and managed to pretend that she hadn't. 'Greg Monteith and I were brilliant, but the audience wasn't the most inspiring ever. We're hoping for better luck next time.'

'Would you care to expand on that?' asked Moira, grinning.

'Not really,' returned Fiona tranquilly. 'I'm dashing off to the Western to see Hugh—and I shudder to think how long it'll take me, without a car.'

'Give him our love' and 'Tell him we miss him' were the most repeatable messages Fiona was charged with passing on when the girls heard where she was bound.

Stopping to buy Hugh a basket of fruit meant missing a bus and it was after seven when Fiona finally found the ward her boss was in. 'In the first of the single cubicles,' returned Sister, when Fiona asked where to find him. 'He's already got his wife and a friend with him, but he'll likely have things he wants to tell you. I know his sort.' Conscientious herself, she had soon identified a kindred spirit. 'And he looks worse than he is. Just thought I'd better warn you.'

Sister had not exaggerated, and, experienced as she was in these matters, Fiona got quite a jolt when she saw Hugh's battered face. She was so taken up with all the scratches and bruises, and the cumbersome Thomas leg splint with all its bits and pieces, that she didn't so much as glance at the vistors.

Battered as he was, Hugh could still talk. 'Fiona— good of you to come. You haven't met my better half yet. Carol, love—this is Fiona Graham, my new deputy.'

Carol was a slim and very pretty redhead. 'We talked on the phone this morning,' she said, getting up and holding out her hand. 'It's good to meet you in the flesh, Fiona.' She was much less agitated than she had been that morning on the phone.

When he got the chance, Greg said, 'Hello, Fiona,' from his seat on the other side of the bed.

'Good grief!' she exclaimed, wondering how she'd managed to overlook him.

'Hugh and I go back a long way,' he explained, having fetched Fiona a chair. 'I thought you knew that.'

'Not from me,' put in Hugh. 'Dropping out of medical school is not something I boast about.' His breath caught in his throat and he coughed, clapping a hand to his side and wincing.

They all reacted in their various ways, Greg asking if he was getting pethidine, Fiona reaching for the sputum carton and urging him to 'cough it up' and Hugh stretching out to cover Carol's hand with his own when her eyes glistened as the tears threatened to spill over.

Then Hugh told Greg that yes, he was getting pethidine and the ward physio was a competent and determined wee soul, so Fiona needn't worry either.

Then a charge nurse came in to give the patient his pre-physio shot and Greg said he'd better be going as he was on call. He looked across at Fiona. 'I could give you a lift if you like,' he said casually.

'You're very kind,' she said just as casually, 'but I've brought some letters for Hugh to sign. . .'

Hugh wasn't taken in by all the play-acting. 'You take that lift, my girl,' he directed. 'You'll have to go in any case when the physio comes. I'm not having you watch me cringe and beg for mercy.' He took the letters and asked for a pen. Then he passed them back, together with some more notes he had made for her earlier. Then he thanked her for the fruit and for coming, and packed her off.

She found Greg talking to a doctor just outside the door of the ward. 'Where's Carol?' he broke off to ask.

'She's staying on for a bit.'

'I thought she would. They're a very devoted couple.'

'I'd gathered that.'

He must have thought she sounded sceptical because he said, 'It still happens—even in these liberated times.'

'Mmm,' Fiona returned doubtfully.

'You're a terrible old cynic, Fiona,' he told her as they made for the stairs.

She definitely did not like the 'old' bit when Deirdre was eight years her junior. 'I prefer to think of myself as a realist,' she returned loftily.

'Same thing, really—depending on your point of view.' He looked suddenly grim. 'You realise that Hugh had a very narrow escape?'

'Yes—I was horrified when Carol was telling me about his injuries. I'd have expected internal fixation of that femur—but presumably it was too fragmented.'

'My conclusion exactly.'

'Haven't you seen the X-rays?'

'No. I may be a power at the City, but here I'm just the patient's best friend.'

'Did you not tell them you're a consultant?'

'One doesn't care to boast,' he returned in a wondrously prim tone, causing her to giggle. 'That's better,' he approved. 'You're a different person altogether when you laugh. More approachable,' he added.

'Most of us are,' she returned. They had gained the car park now. 'Are you really going back to the hospital, Greg? Because if not, you mustn't go out of your way for me——' She stopped. Was she daft? This was not the way to go about cutting out her sister.

Greg came to a halt and looked down at her, his expression baffled. 'I wish I could locate your fast-forward button,' he sighed. 'You keep it far too well concealed.'

Fiona giggled again. 'You certainly know how to make me laugh.'

'So you said last night. And *I* said——'

'I remember what you said.'

'Short-term memory intact, then. I was actually beginning to wonder if we ought to get you seen by somebody.'

'And—I do like you, Greg.'

'Am I hearing aright?' he implored the empty sky. 'Because if I am I might get carried away and enfold her in a steamy embrace in front of this crowd.' He meant a porter and two cleaners who were in quiet conversation some way off.

Fiona giggled some more. 'Do you always exaggerate everything?' she asked.

'I'm not exaggerating my interest in you,' he said softly.

Maybe not, but how exclusive was it? A pity it would be so gauche to ask. . .'I'm flattered,' she admitted.

'And so you should be! I'm much sought after.'

'So I was hearing,' she informed him pointedly. 'It's really astonishing that you're not more conceited than you are.'

'What's that supposed to mean?' he demanded, managing to look rather insulted.

'And to think I've always prided myself on my clarity of expression,' Fiona was saying, when his pager began an insistent cheeping from its home in his top pocket.

His manner changed on the instant. 'Fifteen minutes,' he told it crisply, and then, 'Get in, Fiona—and remember your seatbelt.'

'If it's just a matter of advice, I may not be more than ten minutes,' he said as he parked in his accustomed spot at the City Hospital.

'Not to worry—I can easily walk the rest of the way,' Fiona called after him as he dashed away.

She actually gave it fifteen before going home. She was a bit concerned about leaving Greg's car unlocked, but the park was well away from the main gate and was also overlooked, so it should be all right.

It was a rather disappointed girl who let herself into her flat. What an unsatisfying end to a chance meeting that had seemed to promise so much. She hadn't eaten and presumed that Greg hadn't either, so she'd imagined them laughing together over a meal at the wine bar opposite the hospital. And, of course, undisturbed by any emergency calls.

But life wasn't like that, which was why she had better learn to make better use of such opportunities as did come her way.

Scanning the fridge revealed cheese, eggs, tomatoes and a lettuce on the brink of its sell-by date. Omelette and salad, then. Scarcely gourmet stuff, but nourishing and quick. She had it on the plate when the door phone buzzed. She answered it with a muttered curse.

'Fiona? Greg here. You didn't wait very long.'

'I decided you'd probably be busy for ages,' she returned with a quickening heart.

'If that had been likely, I'd have sent a message. I don't know about you but I'm starving. Come on down and let's go for something to eat.'

She looked at her supper. 'If an omelette will do, why don't you come up?'

'Open the door, then,' he said eagerly.

The second omelette was in the pan and well on its way by the time he rang the doorbell. She let him with a dish-towel over one arm and a bundle of cutlery in her hand.

'You look charmingly domestic,' he said.

'Charm and domesticity,' she echoed slowly. 'Two things I'd never have thought of as going together. Ah, well—this way.' She led him down the short passage to the living-room. 'I'm just about to set the table. Would you like to pour yourself a sherry?' She nodded towards the tray on the sideboard.

'Better not; I've never thought that booze and surgery go together.'

The tables had turned already and she'd thought hers

such a clever opening crack. 'You're right, of course,' she returned quietly.

'But don't let me stop you,' Greg entreated.

'I'm not bothered.' Sudden doubts assailed her. 'This isn't going to be much of a meal, I'm afraid.'

'I like omelettes. And unexpected treats even more,' he added.

Fiona fled to the kitchen, saying she'd not be a minute. She was just in time to prevent his omelette getting past its best. She added a bowl of peaches to the tray with the salad and the omelettes and edged crab-wise with her load down the narrow passage.

Greg went to help her. 'This looks delicious,' he insisted, unloading the food on to the table.

Fiona switched the omelettes round. 'You'd got the wrong one.'

'The one that isn't poisoned?' he queried, laughing.

She laughed too. 'The first to be cooked. It's probably gone leathery.'

'If you say so, but it looks all right to me. You're such a puzzle, Fiona,' he went on without a pause.

'My stepfather calls me enigmatic,' she told him unguardedly. How foolish could you get? 'Why do you think I'm a puzzle, Greg?' she asked quickly, to cover up that gaffe.

'It's the way you keep going back to square one. Once I've softened you up—made you laugh—you're fine. It doesn't last, though, and the next time we meet we have to start again. Why?'

Because when I'm with you I can manage to forget that you're also doing a line with my sister! 'Nobody laughs all the time, do they?' she asked unhelpfully.

'You're misunderstanding me again.'

'Then I'm sorry,' she replied untruthfully, because she'd absolutely *love* to know that she'd misunderstood, and there was nothing at all between him and Deirdre.

'I think I'll have that sherry after all,' she said suddenly, getting up from the table and running over to the sideboard.

'Your omelette will go all leathery,' he warned with his mouth full. His own was already half eaten.

'I don't care,' she retorted.

'So now you're getting reckless. That has to be better than your customary caution.'

Was he laughing at her? Fiona took a hefty swig of sherry. 'Spare me the psycho-analysis,' she begged. 'You'll make me dreadfully self-conscious.'

'How can I?' he asked. 'You're always self-conscious. I think that's a good bit of your trouble.'

Fiona finished her sherry and sat down again. Heavily. That much alcohol on an empty stomach, and her head was swimming. 'You've missed your vocation. You should have been a shrink,' she told him.

'Nonsense! I'm not nearly nosy enough about my patients' darkest, innermost secrets.'

'You seem to be fairly nosy about mine.'

'Only because you attract me so much.'

It was very nearly impossible to believe he wasn't sincere when he looked at her like that. 'You don't beat about the bush, do you?'

'The usual decorous approaches don't work with you, so I thought I'd try something bolder.' He leaned forward to emphasise what he was saying. 'If you really don't like me, you've only to say so and I'll go away. I'd be—very disappointed, though.'

He was pushing hard and in the circumstances she felt that that wasn't fair. 'I—do like you,' she admitted, 'but I need time to—to work out in what way. And how much.' Fiona was proud of that. Drink was a wonderful thing if you took just enough to loosen your tongue without clouding your judgement.

'Yes, you're cautious all right,' Greg had by then

decided. He sounded disappointed. Had he expected her to offer to slip into something loose?

'Would you like some coffee?' Fiona asked politely.

'That would certainly round off this delicious meal,' he returned in similar style. Back to square one, he mimed.

'I'm going to put on the kettle,' she said quickly, diving off to the kitchen.

'What are you doing?' she asked when he crowded after her into the tiny kitchen with the tray of dirty dishes.

'I thought I'd wash these while you brew up.'

'There's not much room in here.'

'I know. Isn't it exciting?'

He was right. It was exciting and she couldn't think of an objection. 'Ah!' she said grimly.

'You were supposed to giggle,' Greg reproved, sighing elaborately. The big breath he had to take to manage such a sigh meant that his diaphragm expanded rather erotically against her left breast.

'Please switch off the kettle—I can't quite reach,' she implored. What she meant was, I can't reach without pressing up against you. . .

For answer, he took her hand and placed it on the kettle switch. 'See? It was really quite easy,' he insisted when the kettle was quiet and they were wrapped fairly thoroughly around one another.

'I think you've taken an advanced course in—in the pursuit of women,' Fiona breathed unsteadily, which was pretty good in the circumstances.

'You're wrong,' he whispered. 'This sort of thing comes naturally when a man is in earnest.' His mouth closed on hers in a kiss that was both compelling and utterly disarming. It was impossible to doubt now that— for the moment anyway—his involvement matched her

own. I'm lost, she realised, I'm drowning. He must care
for me——

That was when that wretched pager went beserk
again. It was in his jacket pocket in the living-room, but
they heard it just the same. 'Blast!' groaned Greg when
he had forced himself to free her.

'The phone's just behind you,' she whispered. 'Perhaps it's only something simple.'

But it wasn't. 'A hit and run,' he said when he'd
checked. 'Of all the luck.'

'Well, I did say I needed time,' Fiona breathed
shakily.

'And now you've got it,' he finished for her. 'I'd
better not come back afterwards, had I?' But it was so
obvious that he wanted her to say yes.

'It's quite late already,' she whispered.

'As you say—well, the junior registrar will be waiting. . . It was a lovely supper, darling. Sorry about the
dishes. . . Oh, hell!'

He went for his jacket, kissed her quickly in passing
where she stood in the kitchen doorway and banged out
of the flat, his footsteps dying away down the corridor.

Fiona honestly didn't know whether she was glad or
sorry about that interruption. When they were together,
it was so easy to believe that she had all his interest. But
now he had gone. . .

Stop it, she told herself. Greg doesn't deserve this.
How can you possibly doubt his sincerity so soon after
such a wonderful time together? Besides, Hugh must
know the sort of man he is, after all these years they've
been friends. He'd have found some way to put you on
guard if he thought it necessary.

'Sorry, little sister,' she said aloud. 'It looks as though
this is one time you'll be losing out.'

* * *

The moment she put her nose round the changing-room door next morning, Fiona was bombarded with questions about Hugh. Rather than repeat herself, she called the whole staff together before they scattered to their various units, to give them the latest news. Then she praised his fortitude and passed on his parting shot. 'And you're all to be very, very good and not give me any aggro, or he'll know the reason why.'

'Good old Hugh!'

'Bless him!'

'Trouble? As if we would!'

'How's Carol taking it?' somebody wanted to know.

'Greg Monteith will look after her,' said somebody else before Fiona could say anything. 'She was his girlfriend first, but Hugh got her in the end.'

That couldn't have caused any acrimony, though, or the two men wouldn't still be friends. How sensibly I'm thinking now, realised Fiona contentedly as she went to the office to sift through the mail.

On the top of the pile was a white cardboard box with a note attached. 'That came by hand ten minutes ago,' said Sharon, who was pretending to tidy Hugh's filing cabinet while she waited to find out who was sending Fiona presents.

'From a grateful patient, I expect,' said Fiona, laying it aside while she divided the mail into 'immediate', 'when I've got a minute', and 'straight in the bucket', according to Hugh's system.

'I don't know how you can,' breathed Sharon.

'I think I hear your phone ringing,' said Fiona in a sing-song voice. Then she relented and called after Sharon, 'If it's chocolates, I'll save you some.'

There were two letters from final-year students enquiring about job prospects at the City. Definitely one for Hugh, who would remember them from their clinical practice sessions here. Next, a long-winded missive which, pared down, meant 'don't be silly, of course you can't have locum cover for maternity leave'. That must refer to Moira. And that means I'll be working on Paediatrics while she's off, and then we'll have to start a waiting list for outpatients. . . Fiona thought.

She forgot all about staff problems, though, when she opened her cardboard box, with the logo of the city's smartest delicatessen on the lid. Who in the world could be sending her smoked salmon sandwiches and the most perfect little fresh fruit salad ever seen? Eagerly she read the card.

> You made a joke of going without lunch, but that's not funny. Hope this will sustain you until dinner. I'll pick you up at seven. PS It's going to seem like a very long day. Greg.

Such thoughtfulness sent her all woozy and weak at the knees. It was, she felt, quite the nicest thing that had ever happened to her, and she didn't mind a bit his assumption that she would drop everything else she'd got lined up in order to go out with him.

'Are you going to be sick?' demanded Dulcie, coming in just then. Dulcie was one of the physios who worked in Outpatients.

Fiona hastily rearranged her face and said she'd only been thinking.

'Then you'd better not do too much of that if that's the effect it has on you. Your first two patients are here—also Mrs Grieve, wondering if you can take her a bit early today as she has to meet a train.'

'I'll try,' said Fiona, stowing away her gourmet lunch in a drawer, to hurry after Dulcie to the treatment-room.

There was nothing like having far too much to do for concentrating a girl's mind. Fiona scarcely thought of

Greg all morning—except when treating one of his patients.

Like Mrs Rintoul, for instance. 'Mr Monteith said that if this treatment doesn't work he'll likely need to remove half ma spine.'

'My goodness, we don't want that, do we?' asked Fiona, making a mental note to check the clinic notes and find out what Greg had actually said. 'So no more slacking about your exercises, madam! Those muscles of yours aren't nearly up to par yet.'

That attempt at matiness only served to remind the patient that she'd got this awful itch round her middle and was Fiona quite sure it wasn't the deep heat that was causing it?

Fiona inspected the rash and said it looked like shingles to her. 'So no deep heat today, Mrs R. It didn't cause this, but it would irritate it, now it's come. This rash is actually due to the same virus that causes chicken-pox.'

'You folk'll blame anything on viruses,' said Mrs Rintoul scornfully. 'I remember once. . .' Fiona let her ramble on while she anointed her liberally with calamine lotion. Then she advised a visit to her GP for confirmation, as diagnosis was not actually a physio's province.

No electrical treatment for Mrs Rintoul meant that Mrs Grieve could be squeezed in early, as she'd asked. 'This painful neck of yours is responding really well to traction, Mrs Grieve. So will you promise me not to be overdoing things while you've got your visitors?'

'Who said anything about visitors, hen?'

'I just assumed—as you're meeting a train. . .'

'Oh, that!' She lowered her voice to explain, 'I don't mind telling *you* that I'm only away to MFI for a new coffee-table, but yon lassie on the desk *talks*, so I wasn't wanting her to know.'

'I see,' said Fiona, who certainly did not. Definitely

another wee anecdote for my memoirs, she thought as she greeted the steel erector patient of Hugh's who had been so stroppy the day before.

'And how are you today, Mr MacSween?'

'I'm nae worse.' Clearly, he'd expected he would be!

'That's what I like to hear,' claimed Fiona.

'You must be stronger than you look,' he decided when Fiona had manipulated him again. 'What did you do to us that time?'

'Just a wee bit of a push and a shove,' she remarked airily. 'Every trade has its secrets.' She never described manipulations in any detail, in case some enterprising patient was tempted to try a sport of DIY, with disastrous results.

'So *was* it chocs, then, Fiona?' asked Sharon, mucking in with the physios to tidy up the treatment-room at the end of the morning.

Fiona frowned. 'Was what. . .? Oh, my parcel. No, just my lunch. Sent in by a thoughtful friend who knows how pushed for time I am. Which reminds me, Sharon. Could you please not bring in more than two new backs at any one time? There wasn't time to assess any of them properly this morning.'

'I only ever slot them in where there's a space on the board,' protested Sharon with a pout. '*Hugh* doesn't mind me making appointments.'

'And for goodness' sake neither do I, just so long as you remember that some take longer to assess and treat than others, such as new backs, any neurological condition, and. . .' Fiona gave up. 'Forget it, Sharon. You weren't to know. Tell you what, when I get a minute I'll make a list of all the most common conditions, together with average likely treatment lengths.'

'I'll be very glad when the boss comes back,' muttered Sharon, flouncing off in a huff.

'And you're not the only one,' sighed Fiona. 'I always

seem to rub her up the wrong way,' she added worriedly to Dulcie.

'Not to worry—it's only the sex thing at work again, and you can't get round that. Believe me, she's had more stringent tellings-off from Hugh for the very same thing.' She cocked an ear towards the waiting-room. 'Is that really the afternoon patients coming in already? I don't believe it!'

The afternoon was virtually a repeat of the morning and when it was over Dulcie said that all she wanted now was a bath and her bed—if only she could find the strength to go for her bus. 'I wish I lived on the doorstep as you do,' she said enviously.

Fiona agreed that she'd been very lucky in that respect. In fact, things are looking up all round, she realised, making the daring decision to ignore the day's accumulation of paperwork for once and go straight home to get ready for the evening.

'Phew!' said Greg, his eyes roaming over her appreciatively from head to toe when she opened the door to him.

'You're out of breath after climbing all those stairs,' she suggested pertly, to cover her excitement.

'I am nothing of the sort,' he retorted. 'I am—how shall I put it?—overcome by the vision of loveliness I see before me.'

'You're out of your century with a phrase like that, but I do like it,' she bubbled. 'It's so much nicer than being told I'm a cracker or a knock-out.'

'You're both as it happens, but I'd never be so crude. Did you get your lunch?'

'Yes, I did—and I meant to thank you so nicely the minute I saw you, but somehow all that eloquence. . . I'm just not used to it. Or to such thoughtfulness. You really are a dear, Greg.'

He grimaced wryly. 'I guess that is an advance.'

'On what?'

'What ever it was you had me down as *before*. No, don't tell me—I'm pretty sure I wouldn't like it. Besides, I've been wanting to kiss you for the past five minutes.' He reached out and pulled her towards him, suiting action to words in a way that left her weak at the knees. 'Am I getting over the doorstep, or are you ready to go?' he asked softly.

It would be crazy to let him in, the way she was feeling after that kiss. 'I'm ready,' she said as firmly as possible.

'And what are you ready for?' he asked teasingly.

Good question! 'Is my memory failing, or did I read the word "dinner" on your charming note?'

'You did, so there's nothing amiss with your memory this time.'

'So where are we going?' she asked when she'd locked the door and followed him into the lift.

'Do you know, I rather fancy a McDonald's,' he claimed.

Fiona raised a saucy eyebrow. 'Why not a Chinese take-away? We could sit and eat it on the steps of the City Chambers. That's definitely the in thing—judging by all the litter.'

'You should have told me before, if that's your idea of an evening out. It's too late now—I've booked a table.'

'At McDonald's?'

'At the Mirabeau.'

'You must have won the pools,' she gasped. Nobody got out of the Mirabeau for less than three figures.

'No—just laying siege to the girl of my dreams,' he breathed in her ear. Silkily. Fiona shivered with pleasure.

She'd never been to that smart and wildly expensive place before, but was eager to know if its cuisine matched its reputation. As course succeeded succulent course, it became apparent that it did. 'I wonder how they make these?' she asked, as perfect little edible baskets filled with fresh summer fruits appeared.

'The baskets? The way they do brandy snaps, only they're moulded round cups instead of the handle of wooden spoons,' Greg explained surprisingly.

'Don't tell me you're a closet chef—I couldn't bear it,' cried Fiona, remembering the simple meal she'd given him the night before.

'I hope I'm not a closet anything,' he retorted. 'I only know about that trick because I asked the last time I was here.'

With Deirdre? 'Laying siege to another dream girl, were you?' challenged Fiona. The wine had been good and she was full of confidence.

'I was giving a birthday treat to an elderly aunt.'

'*What* a lucky aunt,' breathed Fiona, not at all sure that she believed him.

'She thinks so,' he returned, unfazed. His eyes locked on to hers, daring her to call his bluff—if bluff it was.

'With good reason,' Fiona found herself saying instead of the clever disclaimer she'd prepared.

It was one of those places where the table was yours for the evening and they lingered there until almost midnight, laughing quietly sometimes, but always acutely conscious of what was building inexorably between them. By the time they returned to her flat, Fiona had quite forgotten that she even had a sister. And tonight there would be no emergency calls. Tonight, Greg was off duty. 'Coffee?' she offered, for form's sake, when her door was shut against the world.

Smilingly he shook his head. 'No, thanks—I've had enough to keep me going for a week.'

'Me too. I think I've got some brandy somewhere. . .'

'And I've still got to drive home—some time. . .'

'I don't know what else to offer you,' she owned ingenuously.

'Don't you?' he asked, his eyes holding hers, dominating her.

'Oh, Greg. . .' She wanted to plead, Please be honest with me, but she knew she couldn't do it. It was just too naïve. And then she was in his arms and her doubts were swept away on a tide of emotion and longing unleashed by his kisses and the feel of his hands exploring her body.

The phone ringing was like a cold shower. 'Leave it,' he ordered, mouth to mouth. 'A wrong number. . .'

But it didn't stop and in the end Fiona had to accept that only answering it would shut it up. She lifted it off the wall and, 'Where the hell have *you* been?' demanded Deirdre at her most waspish.

'Out to dinner.' Fiona was thankful that Greg hadn't followed her. He'd have recognised Deirdre's voice for sure.

'Till now? Do you know what time it is?'

'What do you want that can't wait until morning?' asked Fiona, ignoring that.

'A bed.'

'What—*tonight*?' A million scenarios, all of them diabolical, filled her mind.

'Don't be ridiculous! You'd have found me camping on your doorstep if it was for tonight! Which reminds me. You'd better give me a key for such times. It's for tomorrow night. I've got an early class on Friday morning and Daddy's seeing a client locally and can't drive me in. And I need to know if you can fix me up, don't I? So as to bring my things. Where were you, anyway?'

'At the Mirabeau.'

Deirdre screamed when she heard that. 'But *I* should

have been there tonight, only he let me down at the last minute. Some dreary old doctors' thing, he said.'

Angry as she was, Fiona could still feel a spark of triumph. Greg meant to take Deirdre, but dropped her to take me instead. . . I'm the one, I *am*! Aren't I. . .?

'Are you asleep?' demanded Deirdre angrily.

'Not quite. You're coming tomorrow, then. I'll try to be home by half-six, only——'

'That's OK—I can't possibly be there before eight. See you then.' Click.

Greg was still in the living-room, staring out of the window at the sparkling lights of the city. He turned around when he heard Fiona's light step and said with a crooked smile. 'So it wasn't a wrong number after all.'

'No—my sister. She wants to come and stay tomorrow night.'

'I didn't know you had a sister—but then there's still so much I don't know about you.' He came swiftly across the room and took her hands.

'And so much I don't know about you,' she countered.

'But we know the essentials,' he returned tenderly, folding her in his arms again.

'D-do we?' she faltered, her eyes wide and serious.

'Are you afraid, darling?' he asked gently, because she was stiff now, not pliant and yielding as she had been before. But Fiona didn't realise that.

'I—don't know. . .'

'I'd never knowingly hurt you. Surely you realise that?'

'People always say that. But they do, though, all the same. . .'

'Not always. Not when it's real.'

'And this—is?' Oh, *why* can't I believe him? she wondered silently. Damn you, Deirdre!

'Yes,' he said, but slackening his hold. 'For me,

anyway. I'm not so sure about you as I was, though. What the hell did that sister of yours say to disturb you like this?'

'Nothing that I didn't—know already,' she whispered.

'Sibling rivalry,' he supposed, and how right he was.

'Among other things.' But she won't spoil this—she won't! Desperately, Fiona wound her arms around his neck. 'I don't want to talk about her any more, Greg. . .'

Gently but firmly he freed himself from her grasp. 'It's clear that I'm way ahead of you,' he said heavily. 'I know what I want, but I don't believe you do. I could persuade you—at least, I think I could—but what's the point if you'd hate us both in the morning?' Then he grinned that crooked grin that was so much a part of his charm. 'A man has his pride,' he said whimsically. Then he kissed her just once, quickly, and then was gone.

# CHAPTER SIX

By MORNING, Fiona had persuaded herself that Greg was in love with her. He must be. Why else had he left her like that last night? He was giving her time, she decided, mooning over a second cup of coffee. He was wonderful, so decent—and just when she'd despaired of ever finding a man like him. He was on call tonight, but tomorrow. . . What would tomorrow bring?

I could cook dinner, she decided as she whirred down in the lift. Cold summer soup—a quick dash across the road—then on with the menu. Would he like poached salmon with hollandaise sauce? That packet stuff was marvellous, just like the real thing. And to follow——

But she never got as far as the dessert. The sight of so many ambulances, lights flashing, streaming through the hospital gates soon dispelled such trivialities as food.

As always, Sharon knew what had happened. 'In the Clyde Tunnel,' she was explaining importantly. 'This great articulated lorry went over on its side and slewed right across both lanes. They're saying that the driver was drunk—and before eight in the morning, too! He must have a terrible liver. Hugh always says——'

But Fiona couldn't wait for Hugh's views on alcoholism. 'Find Marion and the senior on Surgical, please, Sharon, and ask them to come and see me. They'll likely be needing extra help later on.' Though heavens knows how we'll supply it! she thought.

As she anticipated, there was also some spin-off in the main department, too, with several walking wounded sent over from Casualty to be taught the use of crutches, or how to prevent fingers swelling up like sausages while their arms were in plaster.

'Hugh always sends the junior down to A and E for things like this,' said Sharon. 'He says it saves crowding out the department when we're busy.'

Fiona swallowed her impatience. 'For one patient, yes—and it also saves the patient making a detour, but it's not practical when so many patients are involved— and all needing advice at different times.'

The day passed in a blur and but for Greg Fiona would have wished herself back in the comparative calm of her last job. He must be having a hell of a day too. It was a safe bet that a fair proportion of the casualties in an accident of that gravity would have orthopaedic problems.

But he found time to ring her at lunchtime. 'What are you doing?' he asked.

'Eating a chocolate biscuit and trying not to be too rude when replying to a memo from the high heid yin about what he sees as our excessive overtime on ICU. What about you?'

'Much the same, except that his quibble with me is about the cost of all the replacement joints and plates and screws and nuts and bolts I will persist in using. I've just explained that, as far as I'm aware, B and Q haven't yet brought out a cut-price range.'

'Brilliant! You've quite set me up for the afternoon with that. Greg. . .'

'Yes, Fiona?'

'Last night was—wonderful. . .'

'And you've quite set me up with that! Would a quick snack at the winery abut seven also come into the "wonderful" category?'

'Most definitely!'

'See you later, then, sweetheart.' He put down the phone before she could answer.

The afternoon was as hectic as the morning, but now Fiona had something more than a visit from her egocentric little sister to look forward to.

'I don't know how you can be bothered after a day like we've had,' groaned Dulcie, when Fiona admitted that she wasn't going straight home. 'Not *another* heavy date! Where do you get the energy?'

Fiona ignored that and said airily that she was only going over the road for a snack, to save bothering with cooking at home. The grapevine couldn't be on to them yet, and she wasn't going to be the one to feed it.

She got to the wine bar before Greg did and settled into a booth in the darkest corner.

'So we meet again,' she heard him say quite soon, and the words took her right back to the first time they were here together.

'You remembered,' she said, smiling.

'Yes—but I wasn't sure if you did. You were in such a defensive mood that day.'

'Imagine you remembering that as well.'

'I remember everything you've ever said to me.'

'Oh, lord!' she exclaimed. 'That's very disconcerting.' But it wasn't, it was very flattering. And something that was only said to happen when a man and a woman were seriously attracted. . .

They were disturbed briefly when two nurses from Orthopaedics stopped to chat. The speed with which Greg got rid of them was further proof of his interest in Fiona, as well as providing new intelligence for the grapevine. But if he didn't mind, why should she?

They both ordered lasagne and ate it slowly, discussing interests and opinions like two people who'd known one another longer than a mere three weeks. But Greg was on call and had several seriously ill people in his care after the morning's dramatic accident.

When they left the wine bar, she was afraid that he

would suggest coming round later, which would have been disastrous, as Deirdre would be there. When they kissed briefly on parting and he said he would see her soon, Fiona said confidently, 'Tomorrow—you're off duty tomorrow.'

'Tomorrow,' he agreed. 'Or the next day. . .' And tomorrow can't come quickly enough, she thought, delighting in his athletic build and easy grace as he sprinted across the road to the hospital. But before then she was to have a dose of Deirdre. . .

But Deirdre didn't come. Fiona waited until well after midnight before ringing the house, because she didn't want to start a panic. Both her mother and stepfather would go spare if they thought anything had happened to their precious child. But the arrangement had been firm, and Deirdre had now been adrift in the centre of Glasgow for at least four hours.

Fiona was just about to hang up when the phone was eventually answered by Deirdre herself. 'Oh, it's you, Fiona,' she snapped. 'What the devil possessed you to ring at this time?'

Well, I'll be damned, thought Fiona. Is this all the thanks I'm to get? 'Forgive the concern,' she said crisply, 'but you did tell me you'd be here about eight. What happened?'

'I phoned this afternoon and left a message with somebody in your department. Didn't she tell you?'

'Obviously not.'

'The thing is, I'm cutting my early class tomorrow, because nine is the only time the hairdresser can take me.'

'And getting your hair done is more important than your singing?'

'Of course not! Lord, you are a misery—just like Daddy! I have to look my best for the evening, don't I?'

'Because you've got a date with Lambikins, I suppose.' Fiona had only said that in order to hear Deirdre say no, and she was devastated when Deirdre said, 'Who else? He's taking me to that wonderful new place that's just opened in the country, near Busby—to make up for missing the Mirabeau the other night. This is even *more* expensive, but he says I'm worth every penny.'

She sounded so smug and confident that Fiona could cheerfully have strangled her. Or Greg. It didn't really matter which. 'I do hope you enjoy it,' she said sarcastically.

'Oh, I will. He absolutely adores me, you know.'

'Lucky you,' returned Fiona bitterly.

'There's no need to be jealous,' reproved her sister. 'You'll find somebody to dote on you some day. Well, probably. If you're lucky. Goodnight.' She hung up.

Fiona stood there, still clutching her phone. Words were burning into her brain. 'Tomorrow,' she'd said to Greg, and he'd agreed before adding, 'Or the next day.' That hadn't registered at the time, but she understood now. Much as the idea appalled her, he was obviously still seeing them both. And tomorrow was Deirdre's turn!

'What are we going to do about my unit, then, Fiona?' asked the senior physio on Geriatrics. 'I can't manage alone.'

Fiona struggled to drag her mind off her own troubles. The junior was off, then—must be. 'Why not take the student?' she suggested. 'She'd be coming to you next week anyway, and she says she's looking forward to it. And with Hugh off, neither Dulcie nor I have time to supervise her outpatient work as we should.'

'That's a brilliant idea—thanks, Fee. And it's only for one day.'

Of course—the junior was having an interview for a job in his home town, which both Hugh and she were hoping he wouldn't get. He would be such a loss to the staff.

'Fiona, Mr Matthew wants this patient to start treatment right away.'

The man had a grossly swollen hand that looked rock-hard. No wonder! 'All right, thanks, Sharon. Come this way, then, Mr Govan, and tell me all about it. . .'

I'll settle him with some mild infra-red while I fix up Mrs Sharpe on short wave, she thought. *Please*, not another blow-by-blow account of her latest sleepless night——'Mogadon from your GP, Mrs Sharpe? What a good idea. No wonder you look so rested today.'

'Now then, Mr Govan. Was that nice and soothing?'

'Just great, lass. And to think I was scared o' coming here. You hear such things about the way you physios pull folk about.'

By now Fiona had read his notes and knew he'd failed to turn up for treatment immediately after his injury. Now she knew why. 'This is some hand you've got here, so I'm afraid there will be a bit of pulling about. You see, when you damage yourself as badly as this—a vice, wasn't it?—the crushed tissues protest by putting out lots of fluid and if you don't keep the part moving even when it hurts, the fluid goes all sticky and thick and gums up the joints and tendons.' Not an explanation that would thrill an examiner looking for technical terms, but Mr Govan seemed to understand.

'So that's why you're squeezing and pummelling, then. I bet you make lovely pastry, Miss.'

It was rather a good analogy, but Fiona had to shake her head. 'I'm afraid not. I'm too heavy-handed, I guess.' She gripped his wrist with one hand and applied traction to his fingers with the other. There was practically no give, but then she hadn't expected any. If only he'd come for treatment straight away! she lamented silently. Some ultrasound would have prevented this. Now it's probably too late to get complete recovery. Better try, though, as soon as Dulcie has finished with the machine. 'I think some electrical treatment is indicated, Mr Govan. And after that we'll really get down to some loosening.'

He looked alarmed. 'You mean, you haven't yet?'

'Not really—that was just by way of assessing the problem.' And some problem it was, too. If only folk would realise the risks they ran of long-term disability, by dodging treatment in case it hurt. 'Fiona, Miss Pocock from Personnel is on the phone. She wants to know if we really need to replace the juniors who've left, if we're to get more students in the future.'

'Tell her there's quite a difference between qualified staff who can tackle all the simple cases by themselves and students who've had no clinical experience at all, and are here to watch first, and then try a few procedures under strict supervision——No, don't bother—I'd better tell her myself.' Why didn't I have the sense to go in for management? wondered Fiona as she flew to the office phone. It seems to be nothing but a matter of asking silly questions. . .

'And then, apart from the fact that the students we're getting next have never laid hands on a patient before, there's the legal aspect, Miss Pocock. A wrench too far and the patient is paralysed from the neck down, but students are not covered by insurance like qualified staff. The media would have a field day.' Never mind that no second-year student would be allowed near a tricky neck problem, she thought. Go for the image bit; that always gets 'em! Hugh, I think, you'd be proud of me.

'Sorry to keep you waiting, Mr Andrew. A spot of bother on the admin front.'

'Say no more, lass. It's just the same at the factory. These days, the bosses dinnae ken a ratchet from a sprocket.'

Fiona didn't either, but she got his point. Knowledge of the grass-roots processes was no longer a must for management. 'Your range of movement is better,' she pronounced after testing his back.

'Aye, and so's the pain. You and yon Ferguson mannie are a clever pair.'

Fiona thanked him for the compliment and said, 'There's nothing like a bit of manipulation for a back like yours. Ready?'

It went on like that all morning. She'd treat a patient or two and then get called away to the phone, to answer official questions or to speak to a consultant about a patient whose personal view of his progress didn't tie in with his physio's written report. She had to juggle with the timetable because one or two patients were going back to work and needed first- or last-thing appointments. What was that that nervous little Miss Wilkie was calling out? 'No, no, my dear—that's not a peeping Tom—it's the window-cleaner.'

'Lunch-time?' queried Fiona finally. 'Is it really? But I haven't had time to miss coffee yet.'

'You sounded just like Hugh then,' said Sharon.

'Sharon, you've made my day,' responded Fiona, hiding a smile. She hadn't so much as glanced at the mail yet, so she settled down in the office to sort it over a coffee and the cheese and crackers she'd had the forethought to bring with her that morning. She'd no sooner opened the first envelope than one of the juniors looked in. 'We're collecting for some flowers for the boss, Fiona.'

Fiona found her purse and took out a pound. 'OK?'

Back to the mail. A letter from a grateful patient—
always a morale-booster. Especially when the next one
was a thumbs-down to the request for a new tilt table so
desperately needed for the neuro patients. There was
another knock on the door as Fiona took her first sip of
coffee. It was Sally. 'Could I possibly change weekends
on with Gussie, please, Fiona? Only my sister's baby's
being christened that Sunday, and——'

'Of course you can, if that suits you both—but don't
forget to alter the list on the noticeboard.'

'Course not! Thanks, anyway.'

Such scorn, Fiona noted wryly, but forgetting had
been known.

The phone rang at her elbow. 'Sorry, Fiona, but
they'd like a physio on the chest unit immediately and
Charlie's just slipped out to the bank.' Which he had no
business to do without telling me! Fiona thought. 'Say
I'm on my way, please, Sharon.'

Fiona could have sent the junior, but by going herself
she'd score a moral point against the backslider and if
he apologised she would not need to tell him off. She
wasn't very good at that yet.

The patient was just coming to after a light anaesthetic for a broncoscopy. 'And Dr Chalmers insists that
they have some postural drainage just in case,' said a
very new and very self-important house physician.

'If he was sucked out at the time, it's very unlikely
that he'll have anything to cough up and the physios are
due back on the unit in fifteen minutes,' Fiona explained
mildly.

'Dr Chalmers said immediately—and he ought to
know.'

And I don't? Oh, *what* a lovely day I'm having,
thought Fiona, resolving to find out more about this
apparently pointless procedure.

As she'd expected, the patient's chest was quite dry,

and the poor man was not at all pleased to be up-ended and pummelled, all for nothing. Fiona explained that she'd only been doing as she was told, and left him grumbling to himself about inefficiency.

'Fiona! What in the world are you doing up here?' asked Greg, and the sound of his voice set her pulses racing. She took her time about turning round to face him.

'Just answering an emergency call that turned out not to be one. What about you?'

He was frowning at her offhand tone. 'Not back to square one again, surely?' he hoped.

'There are a lot of people about,' she pointed out. And too many for me to deliver that put-down I've been promising you since last night. . .she added silently.

'If that's your problem, then let's slip over the road for a quick lunch. It will have to be quick, though—I've got a clinic in twenty minutes.'

'Sorry, but with Hugh off lunch is a non-event for me most days.'

'I understand. We have to talk soon, though, Fiona.' He opened the lift gates and ushered her inside.

'What about?' she asked as they descended.

'I'm off this evening, but——'

'I know, and so am I. How shall we spend it?' Now let's hear how you wriggle out of that you, you. . .! she thought.

He had the grace to look embarrassed. 'The thing is——'

They'd reached the ground floor and had to edge round two porters who were trying to get a trolley into the lift. It was true, then. Until that moment, Fiona realised, she'd been hoping that Deirdre was making it up. And because it would hurt so much to have him lie to her she said quickly, 'You still haven't told me why you were on that unit.'

'An elderly patient slipped and fell and they were afraid he'd got a fracture.'

'And had he?'

'No, but the poor old chap was badly shaken.' He frowned and sighed and scratched his ear. 'The thing is, I've got this damn date—no, not a date, but something I promised to do weeks ago. And I really can't get out of it.'

Was this the way he'd hummed and hahed to Deirdre before taking her, Fiona, out on Wednesday? Fiona was angry, but not angry enough to ask him that. 'Oh, poor you,' she said silkily instead. 'What is this thing you've got to do—or shouldn't I ask?'

'My elderly aunt,' he said, at which she almost laughed aloud. 'She comes up from the Borders every so often and likes me to take her out. Theatres, dinner and so on.'

'Yes, old ladies do like that, don't they? How very kind and thoughtful you are, Greg!'

He missed the irony completely. 'You've obviously got a few elderly relatives of your own,' he surmised gratefully, taking her elbow and giving it a squeeze, which obliged her to stop walking. 'I tried to get another ticket for you, but tonight's performance is a sell-out.' Another placatory squeeze. 'Believe me, I'd rather be taking you.'

And believe me, I wish I had a hidden tape recorder! she retorted silently.

'You do believe me, don't you?' he asked when she didn't answer straight away.

'That you'd rather take me to the theatre than an elderly aunt? Yes, I think I can manage to believe *that*!'

'Bless you,' he said softly. 'Now then, I'm off this weekend, so what would you like to do tomorrow?'

Was that to be the pattern, then? An evening for Deirdre and then one for her? He certainly fancied himself! 'Sorry,' Fiona sighed theatrically. 'I've got a date myself tomorrow—an old friend. Yes, Fred and I go way back.' Why the devil could I not have chosen a more charismatic name? she asked herself angrily.

'Lucky old Fred,' said Greg, sounding wistful, but not jealous enough to satisfy Fiona. 'OK, it'll have to be Sunday, then,' he supposed.

Given what she knew, his assurance was galling. 'Sorry,' she said again.

'Fred—two days running?' he asked with a frown.

'No, Sunday is for Lance.'

Where was all this drivel coming from?

'And would that be a man or a surgical procedure?' he asked, his eyes narrowing suspiciously. He certainly sounded jealous enough now.

'Lance is all man, I assure you,' Fiona claimed.

'Your life is suddenly very full of men,' Greg said tautly, and then in a milder tone, 'Or is it just that you're upset about tonight? If so, I'll put the old girl off——'

'You can't do that—think how disappointed the poor old soul would be.' She was getting tired of all this play-acting and the strain was telling. 'And as for all the men in my life—well, why not? And I'm certainly not going to—to let them down because, because. . . Anyway, shopping around is not just for men, you know!' And with that taunt she suddenly shot off down a corridor which she soon discovered led to nowhere but the boiler-room. Blast! That had quite spoiled her wonderful exit line. Which wasn't all that wonderful anyway. It would have been, had he guessed she knew about Deirdre, but he hadn't; he'd put it all down to pique on her part. So now he would have her down for either a cheap little flirt or a liar. Fiona couldn't decide which was worse. That meeting hadn't gone at all to plan, but how could she have remained cool and detached when she was hurting so much inside?

If she went on like this, though, Deirdre would win, just as she always did. Unless she got tired of him, but the way she'd drooled on about Greg last night gave Fiona small hope of that.

'We thought you were lost, Fiona,' said Dulcie when Fiona eventually got back to the department.

'So I was. I took a wrong turning coming back from Chests. This place is like a rabbit warren. Think we'll be busy again this afternoon?'

Dulcie said that if they were she would probably go sick, while Fiona scanned her share of the record cards on the desk. 'Oh, help! I'd forgotten this was one of Mrs Morrison's days. The last time I treated her, she said I gave her a migraine.' And, considering it was her knees Fiona had been treating, that was nothing short of slanderous.

'I'll take her if you like,' offered Dulcie. 'But only if I can have this evening off. There's this marvellous man I've just met and I can't find anybody to change with me at such short notice.'

Well, it would be better than sitting at home imagining Deirdre and Greg together. 'All right,' agreed Fiona. 'I suppose it might be worth it.'

The evening was busy, much busier than the time Fiona had deputised for young Sally. Yet still not busy enough to keep her from brooding. I shan't sleep a wink tonight, she supposed as she plodded miserably home. But she'd reckoned without extreme physical exhaustion. . .

Saturday, thought Fiona gratefully when she awoke next morning. No need to rush. She'd stroll round to the hospital presently, catch up on the paperwork, have a light lunch and then visit Hugh. She'd meant to go again before this, but, as she said to him later, the week had sort of got away from her.

'Good grief, girl, you've got nothing to apologise for,' he told her firmly. He was going over the notes she'd prepared so carefully for his information. 'You're showing a wonderful grasp of the job for somebody thrown in at such short notice.'

'Seems more like years,' she returned, 'when so much has happened.' And not just at work either—but it was better not to think too much about that. 'You're off the splint,' she remarked. 'Did they operate after all, then?'

'They did, when I kept on nagging, and now with luck I'll be home in two or three days, and back at work soon after. Not that I'll be much use on the clinical front, but I can at least see to the paperwork. And, before you ask, I have got full flexion of hip and knee.'

'I wasn't going to ask,' said Fiona. 'I didn't dare.'

A few more questions and answers and then Fiona left when Hugh's wife arrived. She was alone, much to Fiona's relief. She'd been afraid that Greg would be with her.

He wasn't far behind, though, and a few moments later they met on the stairs. At first it looked as though he meant to pass her without a word, but after the merest hesitation he said scornfully, 'I hope you had a pleasant evening with Fred,' and then bounded on up the stairs before Fiona could ask after his dear old aunt.

If only he hadn't sounded so damned cheerful! Blast you, Greg Monteith. And as for my sister. . .

To cheer herself up, Fiona went shopping and bought herself a dress she didn't need, couldn't afford and didn't really like all that much. Being crossed in love wasn't only painful; it was also very expensive.

By Tuesday lunchtime, Fiona felt sorely in need of another treat, so she phoned the Royal Concert Hall to reserve a seat for that evening. She didn't know the programme and she didn't much care. If she wanted an evening out these days, it had to be a solo affair and a lone woman was less likely to be groped in a concert hall than in a cinema. Besides, she loved music.

Some time later, when Fiona had just finished treating Mrs Morrison—Dulcie had given her a pain in the neck on her last visit!—Sue Robertson rang. 'Long time, no see, Fiona,' she began unoriginally.

'I know, but with Hugh laid low I've no time for any breaks, never mind a canteen lunch or a fly four o'clock cuppa with you. What news?'

'Oh—this and that.' But she sounded distinctly coy. 'How are you fixed for this Sunday evening coming?'

'I'm free—as it happens.' She'd said that in a convincingly casual manner.

'Great! My place at eight, then—just a few old pals. You'll likely see one or two from school. Nothing special.' Again that coy note, at odds with her words.

Fiona shook her head in puzzlement. 'That sounds like fun,' she said for form's sake. 'I'll look forward to it.'

'You do that,' said Sue with a giggle. 'See you then. Now I must dash.'

They rang off simultaneously, with Fiona thinking that a school reunion had to be better than an evening with the box, or more of that blasted paperwork.

There was a last-minute rush that afternoon, with five patients for immediate treatment coming in together. As Dulcie said, they'd only themselves to blame for drumming it into the doctors that catching things in the acute stage saved time for everybody in the long run.

The patients were all interesting, but especially the young merchant banker called Lance—Fiona had to smile when he introduced himself—a tendo-achilles, ruptured at squash. 'Was I your last patient?' he asked, watching Fiona fold blankets and tidy away equipment.

'Only if I can escape before that phone rings again,' she laughed.

'Then could I offer you a lift?' he asked experimentally.

She would have bet he would offer and she had her answer ready.

'Well, if you should happen to be going anywhere near the concert hall. . .'

'Nothing easier. I'll wait for you in the car park,' he promised.

By the time they'd crossed the city centre, he had asked Fiona out to dinner on Saturday evening and she had accepted. Now all she had to do was let Greg know that Lance was no longer a figment of her imagination — but how?

Thanks to that lift, Fiona now had time for a meal at a nearby restaurant. Things were looking up. She knew a moment's panic when she discovered that tonight's soloist was a celebrated soprano. This was just the sort of concert that Deirdre would enjoy for the chance it would give her to compare the woman unfavourably with herself. So, once settled in her seat, she looked round for her sister and Greg. She couldn't afford to be seen alone, when she'd claimed to have two men dangling after her!

She hadn't spotted them by the time the orchestra began a robust rendering of the overture to *The Barber of Seville*, so she settled down to enjoy it.

Listening to the soloist's flawless account of two Mozart concert arias brought home to Fiona the pointlessness of Deirdre's lofty aspirations, ambitions which their mother encouraged so foolishly. Too much parental love was almost as bad as too little.

Such reflections made Fiona feel almost sorry for her sister, until, gazing round in the interval, she caught sight of Greg's powerful figure striding up the aisle between the front stalls. She couldn't see Deirdre, but then she wouldn't come up to his shoulder, whereas he was fully a head taller than most of the crowd around him.

Fiona slid down in her seat and gave up the idea of a trip to the bar to get a long cool drink. Staying put meant she'd be less likely to be spotted. Yet in way she would have liked them to see her, if only for the satisfaction of watching Greg's embarrassment.

More Mozart in the second half, and then the business of escaping unseen. It wasn't difficult. Greg and Deirdre were in the best seats and would be leaving by another exit. Greg was easily spotted again, while little Deirdre remained hidden in the crowd. Fiona noticed that they didn't seem to be speaking, something that gave her a lot of satisfaction. Was it possible that the relationship with wonderful Lambikins wasn't quite as idyllic as Deirdre insisted?

Saturday was Mrs Crawford's birthday. Fiona had intended posting her mother's present, but the week had been so hectic that she didn't manage to get to the shops until that morning. Two hours at the hospital catching up on the paperwork, an hour searching for something suitable in Buchanan Street, a sandwich at one of the little cafés in the Princess Square Centre and then a long bus ride out to Giffnock. If they were all out—and in a way Fiona hoped they would be—she could leave her gift on the hall table, for she still had a key.

A large caterer's van was blocking the drive, so her mother must be having a party that night. Even with things between them as lukewarm as they had always been, Fiona couldn't help minding that they hadn't thought of inviting her.

She mounted the steps and rang the bell. If they thought of her as a stranger, then she'd behave like one.

'Oh, it's you, Fiona,' said Mrs Crawford when she opened the door. 'Why did you not use your key? I was in the middle of something.'

'Sorry,' said Fiona, reflecting that that word must exceed by millions any other she'd ever used to her mother. 'I only came to bring you this. Happy Birthday.'

Her mother brightened up. 'Oh, thank you, dear—that was kind. And thank you for your lovely card. It came yesterday, but it's very nice.' She unwrapped her present in the vestibule. It was a delicate water-colour of her mother's favourite Hebridean holiday village, which had cost a lot more than Fiona could afford. 'Oh, how pretty. It's very like the one Daddy gave me, but they'll make a nice pair. Are you coming in?' she thought to ask.

'Just for a minute, then, Mother. I'd not want to hold you up if you're busy.'

'So you're not staying for my party, then.'

'I didn't know you were having one and I've arranged to go out to dinner.'

'Yes, you did, dear. I told you—surely. Didn't I?' She looked quite guilty, so Fiona took the blame and said she must have forgotten.

'Is Dee in?' she asked to change the subject.

'No, she's out somewhere—she wants something to wear tonight.'

'I just wondered how she enjoyed the concert last night—presuming she went.'

'Oh, yes—they went. And I gather that Italian woman is getting very shrill in her upper register. Deirdre thinks she ought to retire. She'll be sorry to miss you, Fiona—she thinks a lot of you.'

How is it that my mother can always make me feel

that everything is my fault? wondered Fiona. 'Yes—well. . . I mustn't hinder you, Mother. You must have a lot on your mind.'

'Yes, I have, dear; the caterers have brought some things I didn't order and forgotten most of what I did. The manager's coming any minute to sort it out. You know, you really must come over some time and meet Deirdre's young man. He's a doctor, you know—and we're all *so* pleased with him.'

They must be, thought Fiona, if Greg has graduated from 'a bit older than I'd like' to 'Deirdre's young man'! 'That must be—a great relief. And I'm sure they deserve each other.'

'What a lovely thing to say, Fiona.' Fiona kissed the beautifully made-up cheek her mother presented, thinking, What a bitch I am!

'Drive carefully now,' was her mother's parting remark.

There was no point in reminding her about the car, decided Fiona as she edged round the van. I've never really registered with her since Deirdre was born and I know I never will.

At the gate, she had to leap aside into a holly bush to avoid being run down by a vivid red sports car, swinging into the drive. The catering manager, she presumed. 'Silly man thinks he's Damon Hill,' Fiona muttered furiously as she viewed her scratched hands and ruined tights.

Rather more than twenty-four hours later, Fiona was toning down those scratches with make-up as she got ready for Sue's party. Hen convention or not, she didn't want to look as though she'd spent the weekend fighting.

Her nose wrinkled with distaste as she recalled the night before and its undignified ending. Who would have thought that somebody as apparently civilised as Lance would have gone for such a caveman approach before he was even over the doorstep? He'd apologised—and even sent her flowers this morning, which must have cost a bomb on a Sunday—but somehow she didn't see herself risking another date. And, remembering the energetic way she'd swung her handbag, she doubted that he would either.

She tried on the outrageous dangly earrings she'd bought on impulse while shopping for her mother's present. They almost reached her shoulders and made her look like the sort of girl Lance had obviously thought she was, so she removed them and substituted pearl studs. Next, her best cream blouse, a dark green flowing skirt, matching tights and high-heeled black courts. Oh, yes, every inch the dedicated career girl and the perfect way to look for an evening of gossip with her old school chums. I'm getting rather cynical, she decided as she slipped on a light raincoat against the threatening shower.

But the sun was shining brilliantly by the time Fiona got off the bus at the end of the long, tree-lined road in Pollokshields, where Sue lived with her parents. They had turned the basement into a flat for her—and left her alone to live her own life. 'Just the way your parents do, Fiona,' she'd remarked once, which only went to show how easily misunderstandings developed.

The road was lined with cars for some distance either side of the Robertson gate and the noise floating up from the open windows suggested rather more than the cosy girls' get-together Fiona had been expecting. Nobody heard the bell over all the noise, so Fiona walked in and left her coat in the bedroom, as instructed by a large notice sticking to the hall mirror. Then she followed the noise to Sue's large sitting-room, which was packed to the doors.

'Fiona—*how* marvellous! Not married yet? I am—well, have been. Twice, actually. I mean—all those lovely men to choose from. . .' Stella, the sixth-form siren and not improved with age, it seemed. 'Isn't it heavenly about Sue? Though if I'd seen him first. . .' Fiona let her ramble on, knowing that Stella never required answers.

Somebody thrust a glass into her hand, just as Stella moved on to dazzle one of the orthopaedic registrars. Fiona frowned. If Stella had got it right, then this was Sue's engagement party, and if she'd invited her colleagues, then Greg was probably here. Might even have brought Deirdre. And why not, when he no longer had the hope or intention of ensnaring her own silly self?

That thought was enough for her to drain her glass at one go, to discover that its contents were a whole lot more potent than she had imagined. The effect was to make her wonder if the situation could have possibilities.

By now she had spotted Sue wound round that nice biochemist called Ted, the one she'd said she wanted to discourage. She wasn't too successful, it seems, was the thought running through Fiona's head, when Sue's brother climbed up on a table and confirmed that, though he put it rather differently. There was much clapping and cheering and calls for a toast. Hen party indeed! But then Sue wouldn't have wanted her friends to think that they had to bring a present.

'Have you brought him?' asked a familiar voice about three inches from Fiona's ear.

'Who?' Fiona asked crisply, while willing her pulse-rate to return to normal.

'Lance. Or is it Fred's turn tonight? I wasn't impressed, by the way, that whoever was on duty left you standing at that bus-stop near the concert hall last Tuesday night. I'd have offered you a lift myself, if I hadn't known you must be waiting for him to bring the car round. But why leave you waiting at a bus-stop? After all, a bus-stop is not the easiest place at which to pick up a girl.'

The way he kept saying 'bus-stop' was infuriating. 'I seem to remember you managing it one day,' she retorted crossly.

'It can be done,' he agreed. By now he had noticed one scratched hand and took hold of it to observe. 'Lance certainly lives up to his name.'

Fiona snatched away her hand, furious with him for grabbing the initiative before she'd decided how to deal with him. 'Have you been drinking?' she asked haughtily.

'A little. How else would I have the confidence to speak to such a capricious oddity as yourself?'

'If that was meant to be a joke, I don't think much of it.'

'It wasn't a joke—it was my considered opinion of your character.'

Fiona gazed up at him, her lips moving soundlessly. How did one deal with a man such as he?

'You need a drink,' he interupted maddeningly.

Fiona clenched her teeth and said through them, 'Two would be better if I'm to cope with you!'

'I'm encouraged,' he claimed.

'Because now you can add boozer to your opinion of me?'

'Because now it seems that you're prepared to cope—instead of just mindlessly flattening me.'

'I think I'm going mad,' she muttered on a dying breath.

'I suppose that is the most likely explanation of your behaviour,' he agreed, 'although I'd be very sorry if it were so.'

It was time, and more than time, to call his bluff.

Fiona took a full glass from a passing tray. When she'd half emptied it, she said firmly, 'I saw you at the concert hall the other night,' and watched expectantly for him to wilt.

'Then why did you not speak to me?' he wondered, undeflated.

'Because I didn't think you'd want to be found out.'

Greg's eyebrows almost joined his hairline as he breathed, 'I can't imagine what you're getting at now.'

Fiona emptied her glass too quickly and coughed helplessly. Greg thumped her vigorously between the shoulder-blades, thus increasing her frustration and fury. 'I saw you and that beautiful brunette,' she hissed. She hadn't seen Deirdre, but she had her mother's word for it that she was there. 'She was——'

'With somebody else. I was there alone—thanks to you and Lance,' he added.

'Why deny it?' she asked doggedly. 'I know what's going on. And anyway, why shouldn't you take out anybody who takes your fancy?' Not in the least what she'd set out to say, but she was desperate to trap him into an admission.

But Fiona wasn't the only one whose emotional temperature was nearing boiling-point. Greg fixed her with a look of baffled fury. Then he said deliberately, 'There is only one girl I fancy at the moment, and she is slowly but surely driving me up the wall!'

Somebody then screeched from the doorway that there was supper to be had in the kitchen. The exit surge that prompted separated them and when Fiona looked round for Greg to renew her attack he had left the room.

It was now possible to sit down. Fiona chose the window-seat, where she wilted and stared at the ceiling. She'd been so sure that she held all the aces, yet once more Greg had outwitted her, while keeping his

secret—as he thought. Even his parting shot had been
enigmatic. He could just as well have been referring to
either sister. And yet there were all those times when
he'd really, truly seemed to like her. . . Was it possible
that she could have been so wrong? What a pity one
can't fall in love without losing one's reasoning powers,
she thought. But admitting how she felt about him was
hardly an improvement.

If only she had come clean about Deirdre in the first
place!

'Don't you think my dear little sister looked pretty in
my best dress last night, Mr Monteith?' How easy it
would have been to say something like that on her
second day at the City Hospital. At least then it would
have been a level playing field. But instead she had
allowed an impossible situation to develop.

By now folk were drifting back to the living-room and
Greg might come too at any moment. Having lost all
desire to fight now, Fiona decided to find Sue, offer her
good wishes and get away.

Sue was in the kitchen and at her absolute bubbliest
as she urged her guests to pile up their plates. The
faithful Ted stood beside her, his nice brown eyes
revealing his adoration. Lucky Sue and silly, silly me,
thought Fiona as she wove her way through the crowd
to congratulate them. 'So you did come and you're still
here,' said Sue with less than her usual clarity.

'Yes, on both counts,' returned Fiona with a bright,
determined smile. 'Sue, I'm so delighted for you and I
just know you're going to be very, very happy.'

Sue said that that was the general idea. 'Now you
must tell Ted how lucky he is.'

'I'm pretty sure he knows that already.' Fiona held
out her hand to him, while making suitable comments.
How simple was the mating process when a decent man
knew exactly whom he wanted and went all out to get

her. No woman could resist that. It made her feel so safe and special.

On the way out she saw Greg sitting on the stairs with one of Sue's staff nurses. Even when looking up at her, he could still make Fiona feel small. 'I hope you're remembering that the next sports injuries preventative pep talk is this Thursday coming,' he said tersely.

'I never forget anything to do with my work, Mr Monteith,' she insisted, even though she had forgotten that.

He shrugged and said, 'But then nobody is all bad.'

Fiona didn't flinch. 'I wish I could agree with you,' she returned levelly, 'but unfortunately experience has taught me that's just not true.'

It was as good an exit line as she could have thought of. But she would have given all she had to know that it hadn't been necessary.

# CHAPTER SEVEN

FIONA didn't see Greg for two whole days, which wasn't all that surprising when she was chained to Physio in her role of deputy head. 'And the juniors think that Hugh has a real cushy number,' she moaned to Dulcie at lunchtime on Wednesday. Dulcie was now firmly established as confidante.

'Treating nearly as many patients as we do, pleading our case to Admin, spreading the jam ever more thinly to give every consultant at least some of the input he expects from us, listening patiently to staff grumbles — and as for this——' Dulcie swept a scornful hand over the in-tray on the office desk '—they should try it for a day. Hang on, I think I see silver threads among the gold,' she added humorously, referring to Fiona's blonde bob.

'If you don't, it's only a question of time,' sighed Fiona. 'And to top it all, I forgot to bring lunch again.'

Dulcie conjured a packet of sandwiches from behind her back. 'What a good thing I guessed you would.'

'Dulcie, you're an angel.' She tore open the packet. 'Mustn't get crumbs on this report, though.'

'You're eating too fast,' warned Dulcie next minute. 'Swallowing air and burping at Mrs Morrison this afternoon will not improve things. What did you do to her on Monday?'

'I gave her indigestion—and I've decided to compile a list of the side-effects of short-wave diathermy and strengthening exercises to osteo-arthritic knees. And I'll send it to the *Journal*. The profession must be made aware of the dangers.'

Dulcie was saying what a miracle it was that Fiona could still see the funny side when one of the juniors came in. 'Fiona, is it all right if I leave a bit early today? I've got a heavy date and I'd like to get my streaks re-done.'

'How early is a bit?' wondered Fiona practically.

'About—three?'

Fiona said that wasn't a bit early, it was practically a half-day, and how could she think of it without neglecting her patients?

'I think Angus would give me a hand.'

'Angus has more than enough to do on Ortho, with Pru on holiday,' said Fiona, wondering if Angus was the heavy date. 'You're on Paediatrics, so if Moira can let you go at, say, half-four, then OK. You're not a student now, you know.'

'You can say that again,' snarled the girl, going out and banging the door.

'That one would be better selling Tupperware,' considered Dulcie.

'At least she didn't just disappear,' said Fiona, trying to be fair. 'Oh, lord, is that really the time?' She returned the unfinished report to the in-tray. She would do it at home that evening. *She* didn't have a heavy date lined up.

In a way, she was slightly off course there. She had just finished treating Mrs Morrison—a sore throat today—when Sharon came to tell her there was a man wanting to speak to her. 'He looks like he's from Admin, so I've put him in the office,' she added.

Fiona thanked her, wondering what sort of problem she was to be handed now, and was astonished to find George Buchanan, the banker her mother had urged on her, sitting primly by the desk, feet together and briefcase on his knees. He sprang up and apologised for the intrusion. 'But as I was here visiting one of my more important customers it seemed a good idea to—um— renew our acquaintance.'

Your timing always was at fault, she remembered before saying, 'I appreciate the thought, George, but you've caught me at a very busy time. The boss is in hospital and we're very short of staff.'

'Why not ask your head office to draft in relief staff?' suggested George, showing the deep depth of his ignorance about the NHS. Fiona wondered if he was expecting to be offered tea!

'I appreciate your looking in,' she repeated patiently, 'but I expect you noticed the crowd in the waiting-room. . .'

George said that yes, he had, but as he was here anyway it had seemed like a good idea to look her up.

This could go on for hours, thought Fiona in desperation, so she scribbled her phone number on a scrap of paper and said, 'Give me a ring some time and we'll fix something up. But now——'

'I've obviously caught you at a bad time,' said George, getting the message at last. 'What time do you finish work?'

'Never before six.'

'Because I have go to back to the office to collect some documents which my customer urgently requires. So afterwards, then? I noticed a sort of wine bar——'

'Yes, opposite the hospital gates,' Fiona agreed desperately. 'I'll see you there at half-six. OK?' She bundled him out of the office, saying untruthfully that she looked forward to a chat, and dashed back to her patients.

The next one was a young girl with a severe golfer's elbow, who was very interested in her treatment. 'I don't feel a thing,' she said as she did every day during ultrasound.

'But you are improving. . .'

'Yes, but I don't feel anything.'

'Which is just as it should be,' said Fiona.

'Perhaps if you were to put that queer-looking thing straight on my skin, instead of waving it about under water. . .'

'Then I'd give you a very nasty injury!'

'How can you do that with something that doesn't get hot?'

Fiona decided to baffle her with science. 'To put it as simply as possible, ultrasound in this context works by rearranging tissue molecules—and the results are dire if it's wrongly applied. If I were treating a large area of muscle, then barrier cream and sort of ironing you with the treatment head would be fine, but a bony area needs the underwater approach. Or for a finger, then a bag of water wrapped around it does very well.'

At one time, there'd been a vogue for using condoms and the hallowed walls of St Crispin's had been shaken by the news that Physiotherapy had ordered a gross of the things on their monthly pharmacy list.

'I see,' said the patient, who almost certainly did not. 'So why do you call my trouble golfer's elbow?' came next. 'I've heard of tennis elbow, but——'

'Somehow you've strained the origin of your common flexor tendon,' returned Fiona, cursing those campaigners for freedom of information who encouraged folk to pester overworked professionals. 'Golfers are particularly prone to do that, hence the name. But tennis players put a strain on their common extensor tendon. Got it?' she asked as she switched off the machine.

'No,' said the patient. 'What is——'

But Fiona was already giving deep frictions to the CFT origin on the bony prominence on the inner side of the elbow. 'Hey!' protested the girl. 'That's my sore spot.'

'Because it's the origin of that tendon and frictions are a specific treatment.'

'Don't you have to learn a lot?' said the girl, who'd had all the instruction she could take for the moment.

'So this is what you call frictions, then,' assumed Fiona's next patient, who had been waiting and listening in the next cubicle.

'No, this is called percussion, Mr Barclay,' explained Fiona. 'Your amputation scar healed quickly, but unfortunately, as often happens, some sensory nerve-endings were caught up in the scar tissue—hence the constant irritation you feel. Percussion with this little rubber hammer will gradually numb them.'

'The counter-irritation principal,' he suggested, like an expert.

'You could say that,' agreed Fiona, who felt that she'd done enough teaching for one day.

It was well after the time agreed when Fiona finally joined George in the wine bar. Two coffee-cups and a half-eaten scone were mute witnesses to his long wait.

'So sorry,' she puffed, slipping breathlessly into the chair opposite.

'Waiting ages for you in a place like this fairly takes me back,' George replied.

Fiona wasn't at all sure that that was a good thing when she had no wish to stroll down memory lane and had only agreed to this meeting to get him out of the department. 'I'm very sorry,' she repeated firmly, 'but hospital life is very unpredictable and I've never found my non-medical friends understood——' She broke off because obviously George wasn't listening.

'There's a man at a table near the door and he's staring at me,' he said in a low voice.

'Perhaps he fancies you,' she suggested, quite forgetting that George had no sense of humour.

'Don't be silly,' he reproved. 'Besides, he seems to be with somebody.'

'Then you're probably safe,' said Fiona, side-lining the strange man and getting on with the business of erasing any tender memories George might be cherishing. 'The last time I saw you, you were practically engaged to a nice girl in the same office,' she recalled.

'She married the manager,' said George. 'Besides, she tinted her hair.'

'Just a coffee, please,' Fiona ordered when the waitress came. She was very hungry and would have liked to order some food, but that would extend this encounter. 'And then your mother said something to mine about a farmer's daughter from Ayrshire. . .'

'She was a wonderful cook, but a bit on the heavy side.' George's eyes gleamed. 'You've kept your figure, Fiona.'

'That's hardly surprising when I spend my entire working day at a fast trot.' Having run out of old girlfriends to enquire about, Fiona asked after his sister.

'She's waiting on her divorce. That man is staring again.'

'Perhaps you turned him down for a loan and now he's gone bankrupt. Look, George, would you feel happier if we just left? I ought to be getting back soon—a patient, seriously ill,' she pretended.

'As soon as you've drunk your coffee,' he agreed.

Fiona saw Greg as soon as she turned round to leave. He had also risen, blocking their exit and making introductions a must.

Fiona kept it as brief as possible. 'My colleague, Mr Monteith. An old friend, Mr Buchanan.'

'You must be Fred,' supposed Greg, beginning to believe in him at last. 'Or Lance?'

'You are mistaken,' George answered primly. 'That is

not my name. It's *him*!' he hissed in Fiona's ear, but she'd already guessed that.

'Good God—three of 'em!' exclaimed Greg. 'And you've the nerve to accuse *me* of leading a double life.'

'I don't like your manner—or your tone,' said George before seizing Fiona's elbow and towing her on a detour to the door. 'A colleague, you said,' he recalled as they crossed the road to the gates of the hospital. 'More like a patient, I'd have thought—and a mental one at that!'

Fiona instinctively defended Greg, which should have told her something about her feelings towards him, if she hadn't known them already. 'It makes perfect sense in the proper context, but would take too long to explain. So nice to see you, George, and I'm sorry I kept you waiting. . .' She was havering. 'And now I'd better dash. . .' She was desperate to get away from George before Greg came out of the wine bar.

'So had I,' said George, on his dignity after what he saw as the brush-off. 'Mother worries when I'm late.'

'Remember me to her,' called Fiona, backing thankfully away through the gate, then peering through the railings to make sure he went to his car and drove away. Then she emerged from her hiding place to go home.

She met Greg head-on, on the very spot where she'd held him up on her first day. She was shaken, but he appeared to be completely unfazed as he said briskly, 'Eight tomorrow at the Olympian Club. I take it you know where it is?'

'It's that big mansion place next to the Botanic Gardens.' Every Glaswegian knew that; it was said that you had to make your first million before they'd let you join. Fiona remembered something else. 'Is it not a strictly men only place?'

'It is, but you're visiting in a professional capacity— they have waitresses and cleaners, after all.'

'Thank you—I'm very relieved,' said Fiona. 'I'd hate

to find myself bawling information through a mega-
phone from the car park—or the kitchens!'

She thought that was a wonderful bit of repartee, but
he showed no appreciation. 'It would have been much
better if I could have taken Hugh to that particular
location, but it's much too soon—although he did offer.'

'How like him!' Fiona said warmly. 'I'm afraid I
haven't seen him since he went home, but——'

'You're doing your bit if you manage to keep things
ticking over here,' he cut in impatiently. 'And he hopes
to be back early next week.'

'Splendid,' she said. 'I'm not too good at dealing with
difficult staff.'

'Really?' Greg was amazed. 'I'd never have thought it
when you're so aggressive in your personal life. Eight
tomorrow, then—and please don't be late. I'm playing
squash afterwards.' He then strode off towards the car
park, leaving Fiona staring after him. He'd never
spoken so tersely to her before; not even at that first
unfortunate meeting. Still, what else could she expect?
She'd found him out in deceit and called his bluff—and
no man took that lying down. Especially if he deserved
it. It wasn't in the nature of the brute.

When Fiona cut across the chatter in the staffroom next
morning to announce that the boss would be back within
the week, a great cheer went up. Complimentary
remarks flew about and the girl Fiona had turned down
for time off the day before said at least you could always
rely on Hugh to be fair.

'Don't let her get to you,' advised Moira. 'Besides, it
was I who actually said no——'

'Fiona, would you please ring Ambulance Control?'
interrupted Sharon. 'They say they can't bring Mrs
Irvine in today and they'll take more notice of you

telling them that Hugh says they *must* come in daily if they're having CMT.'

'CTM—connective tissue massage,' Fiona corrected automatically. 'OK, Sharon, I'll have a word, and if they still say no I'll try for a Red Cross car.'

'Did you persuade them?' asked Dulcie when Fiona joined her a few minutes later in the big treatment-room.

'No, I didn't. They've got three vehicles off the road, but the car service will try to squeeze her in this afternoon. God bless the voluntary services. Oh, hello, Mr Tait. You're early.'

'I've got an interview for a job,' he said jubilantly. No wonder he was looking smart enough for a wedding. 'I'll not be mentioning my back, though—no sense in ditching my chances.' He looked round at all the patients already there. 'I could give it a miss the day. . .'

'No, in you go. Twenty minutes should sort you out.' He had wrenched his back and spent weeks going to a quack until his money had run out. This would be his fifth progressive manipulation here and already he was almost pain-free.

'You should advertise, lassie,' he said when she'd put him through his paces with the usual good results.

'That's forbidden,' returned Fiona, laughing. 'The Health Board would go mad.' Though sometimes I wonder if they haven't already! she thought to herself with a smile. 'Well, good luck with the interview, Mr Tait. I'll be keeping my fingers crossed for you.'

'Fiona!' Sharon again. 'That's Sister from Urology on the phone now. She's done something to her neck, but she's too busy to see about it and wonders if you could fix her up with a collar pro tem?'

'Tell her I'll be along as soon as I possibly can. . .'

'Now this is only a stop-gap, mind,' she told Sister earnestly some time later. 'I'm glad you're comfortable, but you must get an orthopaedic opinion, and if you don't promise I'll jolly well report you.'

Sister said, All right, then, she'd pop down to A and E as soon as she got a minute.

As soon as she got back to Physio, Fiona was accosted by a very angry young woman. 'Are you in charge? Then I wish to complain under the Patients' Charter. My appointment is for eleven and it's now nearly half-past.'

'Yes, please do complain,' urged Fiona, taking the wind out of her sails. 'We're currently two physios short on Outpatients alone, and the caseload is increasing daily. Did you report to Reception?'

'Why would I? They knew I was coming. Now see here, I start work at twelve and it's a long bus-ride.'

Not till twelve? Lucky you, thought Fiona wryly as she went to ask Sharon to look out the girl's record card. Oh, God—another back. What was Sharon thinking of, bringing her in at the busiest time. A forceful miss, though. She would have browbeaten Sharon, perhaps. . .'How did you injure yourself?' asked Fiona as the girl was undressing.

'At work.'

The space on the card for occupation was blank. 'So your work involves heavy lifting, then, does it?'

'No. One of the punters tried to pull me off the platform.'

'Surely you're not a railway porter?'

'For heaven's sake!' exclaimed the girl irritably. 'I'm a go-go dancer and I fell when this guy got hold of my leg!'

'Yes, I can see how it happened now,' said Fiona, thinking that there was always a first time. 'The x-rays show no bone damage, but there's a bit of muscle spasm still, so three or four applications of deep heat and some stretching exercises should sort you. . .'

Fiona had often noticed that a day which began badly seldom improved, and that Thursday was no exception. She spent rather too much of it apologising to patients for keeping them waiting. 'I think I'll record a message and play it in the waiting-room every half-hour,' she told Dulcie when the last patient eventually left at half-six.

'Scot Rail could advise you on the format—heaven knows, they've got enough experience,' said Dulcie, who travelled in and out by train daily.

That reminded Fiona of her mistake about the go-go dancer's profession and they chuckled over that for a moment. But they were soon grumbling again. 'What really bugs me,' said Fiona, 'is that we always come out looking so inefficient, when most of the time it's somebody else's fault. Take Mrs Irvine. The ambulance couldn't bring her this morning, and so when she came in the afternoon we had to keep others waiting for ages, so as not to mess up the car driver's schedule—when he was doing us a favour.'

'Never mind about taking Mrs Irvine—take a couple of aspirins,' advised Dulcie. 'You've got to present physio in the best possible light tonight. Or had you forgotten?'

'No—and I never felt less like beating the drum in my entire life.'

'You had the foresight to dress up a bit today, so you don't need to dash home. Take a leisurely shower here and go over the road for a nice salad. That should help to restore you.'

Fiona said that Dulcie was a genius and she would follow her advice to the letter. Unfortunately, the wine bar was having the sort of day that they'd had, and it took so long to get served that only taking a taxi would get her to the club on time.

Greg was parking his car when Fiona arrived and his

greeting didn't improve her temper one bit. 'Physios must be better paid than I thought if they can swan around the city in taxis,' he observed infuriatingly.

'I have had one hell of a day and it was either a taxi or being late. And you ordered me to be punctual,' she reminded him grimly. 'Of course, if I hadn't bothered to *eat*, I could have caught a bus, but as I'd had no lunch I thought I'd better have something. I don't imagine you'd have been thrilled had I fainted in the middle of my spiel!' And now, of course, he would think she was playing the martyr.

'I'm sorry,' he said—and he actually sounded it. 'I should have remembered how busy you must be with Hugh away.' So he wasn't dead set against apologising, then—just so long as it wasn't about something really important!

'Yes,' she returned crisply. 'Unlike a lot of superintendents, Hugh treats a lot of patients.'

'I thought he only took a few cases to keep his hand in.'

'He does a lot more than that and if he didn't we'd never get through the work. Did you know that the last two juniors to leave haven't been replaced yet? And the first left six months ago.'

'I never knew that!' exclaimed Greg. 'I suppose Hugh didn't want to presume on our friendship. You can rest assured I'll take it up with the chairman at the next consultants' meeting.'

'Thank you,' said Fiona, but without much hope. Hugh had told her more than once that the unit general manager suspected everybody of empire-building if they so much as uttered the word 'staff'.

She followed Greg up the steps. He opened a massive front door and ushered her into a huge panelled hall carpeted in inches-deep Wilton. When the desk clerk rushed forward, his mouth hanging loose at the sight of a female intruder, Greg explained who they were. They were then taken to a large room, where men of all types and ages were sitting round in deep leather chairs, calculated to give the fittest present backache. They all had a glass of something or other and Fiona observed wryly under her breath that they all appeared to be safe from activity-induced injury at the moment.

'All the same, it would be interesting to know their incidence of heart disease and strokes,' Greg returned in the same undertone.

But despite unfavourable first impressions this turned out to be a much more rewarding evening than their last excursion into preventive medicine. The club members, though relaxing now, were genuinely interested and the questions that followed the talks were very much to the point. Fiona and Greg were then invited to inspect the club's own gym and when several members expressed an interest in hospital methods and equipment Fiona offered to lay on a demonstration in her department.

Questions were resumed and when it got to the point where it seemed that they were never-ending a man stepped forward and thanked them most encouragingly for their stimulating and informative talk.

'Quite a difference from the last time we went into the education business,' remarked Greg in a low voice, just as a personable young man in a dark business suit came up to them, his eyes fixed curiously on Fiona.

'Excuse me, Mrs Graham,' he said courteously, 'but haven't we met before?'

Fiona saw no reason to embarrass him by correcting him about her marital status, so she said with a smile, 'I don't think so. For one thing, I've been out of Glasgow for some time and have only just returned.'

He wasn't convinced. 'Do you know, I could have sworn you were my boss's elder daughter?' he persisted.

'He gave a Christmas party at his home about two years ago and all his family were there.'

Fiona didn't remember him at all, so she replied, 'I'm sorry, but it couldn't possibly have been me. My father died when I was four years old.'

'I'm sorry, too,' he went on, as people often did in such circumstances, 'but the likeness is extraordinary. I could have sworn you were she. Perhaps you're related,' he compromised.

Fiona was beginning to feel sorry for him. He'd made a mistake and couldn't bring himself to admit it. 'I suppose that's possible,' she allowed kindly. 'Family resemblances are—quite fascinating.' She then went for a change of subject and asked him what his particular sport was.

He said, 'Squash,' and immediately returned to the attack. 'I'm a junior partner in Crawford and Morrison, the law firm in Bothwell Street,' he said devastatingly. 'John Crawford has two girls with quite a gap between them and——'

'That is very interesting, but my father is dead,' Fiona repeated desperately. The man was right after all, *and* he knew it, but he must be stopped. What could Greg be thinking? She didn't dare look at him. 'If there is a blood relationship between your boss and myself, then I'm not aware of it. Sorry!'

'So am I,' he returned stolidly. 'Well, please accept my apologies. I enjoyed your talk very much,' he claimed belatedly, before losing himself in the crowd.

'What an extraordinary coincidence,' said Greg, eying Fiona intently.

It was a chance to clarify things but she hadn't the courage. 'More a case of mistaken identity,' she returned. 'Excuse me. . .' She turned eagerly aside, blessing the man who had come up to her wanting to know in more detail why she placed so much emphasis on getting an ice-pack on to a soft-tissue injury as soon as possible.

By the time she'd finished her explanation, somebody else had buttonholed Greg. This was surely her chance to escape before Greg could probe further, as instinct told her he meant to do. Sue had told her a while back that he knew Deirdre had a sister who worked at the City Hospital.

By good luck, the man who had chaired the session was free and getting himself a drink from the bar. 'What'll you have?' he asked when Fiona appeared beside him.

'Nothing, thank you—I just wanted to say that I have to leave now. . .' She was breathless and rather flushed, and the man looked at her curiously, puzzled perhaps by the contrast with the cool and capable girl who had spoken so confidently earlier.

'Well, if you must, you must, my dear,' he agreed. 'And we'll hold you to that demonstration you promised us.'

'Oh, certainly—just as soon as I've cleared it with the general manager.'

She hadn't quite reached the front door when Greg caught up with her. 'I thought you were staying on to play squash,' she quavered as all her apprehension resurfaced.

'I changed my mind. I want to talk to you.'

'You think I was wrong to suggest that demonstration,' she blurted out, clutching at straws. 'But I felt I had to. It didn't take a minute to see that they hadn't a clue about the correct application of any of that complicated and madly expensive equipment. And misuse can do as much, if not more damage to muscles than occurs in the course of strenuous activity. And then when I heard that man say that they were thinking of buying some ultrasound machines I nearly died! They're obviously not short of money, so I wonder why they don't employ a physio? Um, you wanted to say something,' she caved in, the third time he opened his mouth to get a word in.

'I certainly do! Somebody on the committee came up with the idea of offering you a job and in two seconds the idea was proposed, seconded and carried. I came hurrying after you primarily to warn you.'

She didn't dare to contemplate his secondary reason. 'If they do, then I shall certainly give it some thought,' she insisted. 'It might be quite a good job. No night calls, no weekend intensive care stuff.' How long can I keep this up? she wondered. 'And some of those men looked decidedly—well—interesting.'

Greg's upper lip was curling in disgust. 'That was a very cheap remark,' he said heavily. 'And I doubt the hours would be as regular as you seem to think. Businessmen will want evening and Saturday treatment—especially as they'll be paying for it. There could be other complications, too. There are some fairly dyed-in-the-wool chauvinists in this club.'

'Then I should feel quite at home after six years in hospital,' retorted Fiona. 'Anyway, I thought they treated me very courteously.'

'You were under my protection,' he returned smugly.

'Huh!' she snorted.

'And what of that lawyer who thinks that he works for your father?' he said pointedly.

'That was all rubbish,' was the best she could do. 'Now if you'll kindly excuse me, I think there's a bus due about now.' In fact, she had no idea about that, but the conversation was getting critical again. By now they'd left the club and were standing by his car.

'I'll take you home,' was the way he dealt with that. 'Curious, though, wasn't it? He seemed so sure he knew who you were.'

'And you think I don't? He got it wrong!' she insisted, which he had in part. 'As far as I'm aware, I never saw that man before in my life.' And that was true, though small comfort. 'I'm glad things went better tonight, but please, I really want to go now. It's been a very long day.'

'You must let me drive you.'

'No—not when you live so close by.'

'And you're only so far from home because you were helping me.' He unlocked his car. 'Get in, please, Fiona.'

He could mean well, but he would almost certainly dig deeper if she complied.

'Thank you, but I really prefer not to trouble you.'

'I understand,' he said quietly.

'I'd like to think so,' she returned uncertainly.

'I do,' he insisted. 'I understand very well—and rather more than you think. Goodnight.'

# CHAPTER EIGHT

'NOT finished yet, Fiona?' asked Angus at one o'clock on the following Saturday.

'Almost. I'm trying to leave everything up to date for the boss's return on Monday.'

'You've had a hell of a fortnight,' he sympathised.

'Not as bad as Hugh's, I'll bet! Any problems on the wards, Angus?'

'Not to my knowledge, but the duty weekender is still on ICU. Er, is it all right if I——?'

'Go now? Sure—and have a nice weekend.'

'You too.'

'Thanks, I will,' Fiona responded automatically. Yes, it would be a super weekend—of washing, hoovering, re-stocking the fridge. Thinking. . .

She'd been over and over that exchange with Greg in the car park at the Olympia Club last Thursday and always with the same result. Until then, she'd had the upper hand. He'd deceived her and she'd let him know she knew it. But now he knew that she'd deceived him too—and in two respects. From his point of view, he'd done nothing worse than date two girls at once. But she, on her own admission, had been juggling four different men simultaneously. The fact that she'd invented two of his three 'rivals' in order to get even was immaterial, because he didn't know that. Add to that the little matter of concealing her relationship to Deirdre, and it was difficult to see how things could possibly be worse.

They could, though.

'I'll be in all afternoon if there are any unforeseen problems,' Fiona told the duty physio before leaving the

145

hospital, so when she heard the phone ringing as she unlocked her door she naturally expected to hear the girl's voice.

'Fiona, how could you?' cried her mother in an anguished voice before Fiona could say anything.

'How could I what, Mother?'

'Deny Daddy like that, after all he's done for you. And to one of his juniors, too. You're a wicked, ungrateful girl!'

Oh, lord—she should have foreseen this; should have realised that that bright young lawyer would have to prove his point. 'But I didn't, Mother. At least. . .' She tried to remember exactly what she'd said. 'I told him there was no blood relationship, which is the truth. As I remember, we'd been talking at cross-purposes and I didn't know who he was. And——'

'Why did you not tell him that Daddy is your stepfather?'

'It wasn't exactly straightforward and—and Deirdre's boyfriend was there! He didn't know who I was and I didn't know whether you'd want me to be the one to tell him. I'm very sorry, Mother. I was only trying to save more embarrassment all round. He'd called me *Mrs* Graham you see, and——'

'Who had? Peter?'

'Is that his name? We weren't introduced—he just came up and we started talking. I see now that I made a dreadful mess of it and I'm terribly sorry. I never dreamed he'd say anything to Pa—I thought we'd got it straightened out. I'm so sorry, really sorry,' she repeated, and so she was. In trying to keep Greg in the dark, she'd unwittingly wounded her stepfather who had, as her mother insisted, been good to her.

'I'll write to Pa and apologise and explain how it all came about.'

'That's the least you can do! I'm so vexed with you,

Fiona—shaming us like this. . .' Fiona stood and took as much of that as her mother wanted to deliver. For once, she felt, Mother had right on her side.

But at last Mrs Crawford could rail no more, and with a final word of apology Fiona thankfully rang off. She then sat down to draft that letter. It was depressingly difficult and her waste-paper basket was soon overflowing. But at last she managed to produce a clear account of her meeting with the forceful Peter and her reasons for saying what she did, and that without making herself look either ungrateful or a complete idiot.

She walked all the way to Bothwell Street and dropped it in the mailbox at Pa's office. That way he'd get it as soon as possible, and have a chance to read it in peace without her mother fussing curiously over his shoulder.

As eagerly anticipated, Hugh came back to work on Monday and Fiona gladly relinquished the reins. 'So you didn't enjoy being the boss, then,' guessed Hugh from the warmth of his welcome.

'No, I did not. In fact, I'm cured of all ambition in that direction.'

'You'll see it differently if you're ever in danger of finding yourself working under somebody younger than yourself.'

'As Marion is placed now,' she remarked.

'Ah, Marion,' he sighed. 'Now she's a different person altogether.' He opened another letter. 'Good lord! Personnel are advertising those junior posts at last. What did you say to make 'em agree to that?'

'I just painted rather a lurid picture of unsupervised students running amok with disastrous results. I can't believe they actually fell for it, though.'

'Well, something has dislodged the proverbial finger. You did well, Fiona,' he summed up. 'And I'm very grateful. And now will you look at what's just blown in?' he said as Greg came into the office. 'So what miracles are you expecting from my overworked staff?' Hugh demanded of his friend.

'I don't care how unethical this is,' Greg answered grimly, 'but I intend to satisfy myself that those clowns at the General were right to allow you back to work. So kindly drop your breeks.'

'Careful,' warned Hugh, with a broad grin. 'That's the sort of request that can land a man in deep trouble. Not a word of this outside this room, Fiona.' He seemed quite unaware that his deputy and his friend were carefully ignoring one another.

'You can both rely on me to keep my mouth discreetly closed at all times,' she declared, going out and shutting the door. That had been intended to let Greg know that she'd not be blabbing to her sister about his double-dealing, but he probably hadn't got the point. She wasn't good at managing tricky situations. Look what a mess she'd made of that encounter with Peter Thingummy.

'I thocht I haird yon lassie at the receptacle say that Mr Ferguson was back,' said Miss Simpson, when Fiona invited her to get ready for treatment in her usual cubicle.

'That's right, but——'

'Then why is he no' treating me?'

'Because he's restricted to office work only for some time. It's only a few weeks since his accident and, among other things, he broke his leg rather badly.'

'And I broke ma shoulder—or so they say.'

'That's quite different, though.'

'A break's a break, whatever.'

As briefly as possible, Fiona explained the relative gravity of a fractured shaft of femur, compared with Miss Simpson's injury.

'Aye—well, I still say ma eyes is more trouble.'

'No movement on that front yet, then?'

'O, aye—I'm seein' the TNT man next week aboot ma glasses.'

'Good,' said Fiona, who'd tried more than once to sort out that particular misconception and didn't feel up to trying again. 'And with your shoulder almost A1 now, that's one problem the less.'

'I'd rather get ma nose cleaned out,' declared the patient.

Dissatisfied customers apart, it was quite a good day, with nothing to do but treat patients, one after the other, or even several at once now and again.

Meanwhile, Hugh was dealing with all the queries and admin. 'Your leg is painful,' realised Fiona as she saw him pop a couple of pills into his mouth when she took him a late-afternoon cuppa.

'A bit. I think it's this damned chair.'

'But of course! It's completely unsuitable. What's the matter with us, Hugh? If you were a patient, we'd have sorted it right off.' Fiona rushed away and brought back one of their few firmly upholstered chairs of the right height, plus a pillow and a leg-rest. Then she fussed him into position with repeated warnings about bending and stretching his knee for five minutes every half-hour.

'I can't be bothered with all that claptrap when I'm busy,' grumbled Hugh, sounding exactly like a patient. 'Anyway, I'm going home in a minute. Carol's teaching this afternoon, so Greg's taking me on his way to the medical school. That's good tea, Fiona. I'd not say no to another—and Greg could probably do with one too.'

'I'll make a fresh pot,' she promised, resolving to get one of the others to take in the next tray.

Even so, she didn't manage to avoid Greg. 'Hugh says to tell you there's a call for you on the office phone,' said Sharon.

'Thank you,' said Fiona, hoping it wasn't a personal call.

It was Lance, newly back from a business trip and anxious to make a fresh start, as he put it.

'Ah!' said Fiona, causing Greg to cast a satirical look in her direction.

'You don't sound very encouraging,' said Lance carefully.

'I was in the middle of a treatment,' said Fiona even more carefully.

'Would you rather I rang you at home, then?' he asked.

She would rather he didn't ring at all, but saying so in front of Greg would put her in the wrong for receiving a personal call during working hours. 'That would be better,' she agreed.

'Then tell me your number—you're not in the book.'

'Ah!' repeated Fiona. 'It might be best if I contact you when I'm not busy. Thanks for calling.'

'I must say, you're very offhand with your admirers,' teased Hugh as she put down the phone.

'How do you know that wasn't a patient calling?' she wondered.

'Because he asked to speak to his friend Miss Graham.'

'Ah! Well, I don't think he'll ring again in working time.'

'I'm sure he'll not. If only all hospital staff were as meticulous as you, my dear. Practically perfect, my new deputy,' Hugh told his friend.

'Ah!' exclaimed Greg, far more emphatically than Fiona ever had.

She gave him a long, wounded look and hurried out of the room.

Next morning, Marion phoned in to say that her mother's daytime carer hadn't turned up.

'I told her to take as long as she needed to get things on a firmer footing,' said Hugh to Fiona. 'This could be the chance we were looking for.'

Blast, thought Fiona. A stint of Orthopaedics just now was the last thing she wanted. She pointed out how busy they were in the department and Hugh solved that, in part, by saying that young Angus could work there mornings and go to the wards in the afternoons.

To argue would only make him wonder about her reluctance. 'OK, I'll be off, then,' she caved in.

'Great!' cried Sue when she saw her friend. 'You'll soon have them all up and running.' She then gave Fiona a quick résumé on the most pressing cases and an update on those few she would remember from her last spell on the unit, almost a month ago.

'Presumably he got married,' said Fiona, referring to the bridegroom victim of the post-stag-party crash.

Sue smiled at the recollection. 'He certainly did! His mother-in-law saw to that, turning up with bride, cake and minister on the following Saturday. No second thoughts allowed there!'

Fiona looked slightly alarmed. 'I don't like the way you said that.'

'Don't worry. I'm not having second thoughts,' Sue quickly assured her. 'Pencil in the eighteenth of September in your diary—and fail to turn up at your peril!'

Fiona said Sue could rely on it and hurried off to start work before Sue could ask for details of her own love life.

The afternoon would see Greg's weekly ward round, so Fiona resolved on a quick round of her own, so as not to be caught napping. That done, she got down to some serious treating. 'And you can believe that's the last time I accept a lift,' declared Mrs Fulton when she'd finished telling Fiona how she came to be lying here in this bed with a head harness 'and all these weights stretching ma neck till it matches the length of ma legs', as she put it.

Fiona agreed that that might be wise, but pointed out things could have been worse. 'You could have sustained a fracture or two.'

'Or nothing at all if I'd walked to the shops. How long will I be left like this?'

'Until the irritation to the nerve-roots in your neck has subsided and you're pain-free.' And that'll not be just yet, Fiona added to herself, having detected definite weakness of grip in Mrs Fulton's left hand. 'Did Miss Brown give you anything to squeeze?' she asked.

Mrs Fulton's face creased in a broad grin. 'No, but if I'm to get a choice I'll take that nice young colleague of yours—Angus as they call him.'

Fiona said with an answering grin that she was very sorry, but he was working in Outpatients at the moment, and Mrs Fulton would have to make do with a light spring grip.

Next came more chest checks and reminders about movement for all patients operated upon in the past few days. Then lanolin massage for three skin grafts.

One patient must have thought she was using glue. 'Would it no' stick down of its own accord, then?' he asked.

Fiona explained that it was more a matter of keeping the grafted skin supple and soft while it got used to life in its new situation. She'd developed a store of such simple explanations over the years and found that they went down better than anything too scientific.

Her eye was caught by an old man hirpling past with a walking frame which was much too big for him. 'Just a minute, Mr Polwarth,' she called out, having spotted the name on the Zimmer's label.

'If you mean me, the name's McCorquodale,' she was firmly informed.

'But it says there. . .'

'Borrowed, lass. It's newer than mine, ye ken. Now, oot o' ma way. I'm wantin' the lavvie.'

For his return journey, Fiona went to find his own frame, and on the way back she explained the importance of having one the right height. 'If it's too high, you can't get the same pressure on it with your hands, and if you can't do that, then you can't take enough weight off your gammy leg.'

'Legs, lass—not leg. I've busted 'em both at different times and now this thing of mine is clean worn out.'

'I noticed,' said Fiona, wondering why Marion hadn't, 'and I'll be bringing you a new one later on.'

'Now ye're talking stuff I can understand,' was the response.

Having allowed herself to get side-tracked, Fiona wondered if she would manage to get all the most pressing cases seen, if not actually treated, before the round.

She did, but only by going without lunch. So at least he can't find fault with me on the professional front, Fiona thought complacently as she joined the team assembling in the office. Greg was there already and he gazed at her in surprise and distaste. 'And where is Marion?' he asked.

To her deep annoyance, Fiona felt her colour rising in response to that look. 'She's having problems at home again and I'm deputising,' she returned stiffly.

'I see.' He looked her over again. 'Then you must be very busy, so I'll excuse you from the round. Besides, you wouldn't be able to make much contribution, would you? If anything crops up relevant to physio, we'll let you know.'

Fiona was hurt and furious in equal measure. Damn

you, Greg Monteith, I went without lunch to be ready
for you, she wanted to spit at him. But he had already
turned his back on her to speak to the houseman.

And he wouldn't have cared if she went without food
for a week. They'd slipped back a long, long way from
the point at which he'd had that wonderful lunch
delivered to her from the smartest delicatessen in town.

That afternoon, Fiona tackled her work with a strenu-
ousness that startled and galvanised the patients into a
matching response. 'I wish I could get them to work half
as hard for me,' said Pru enviously when Fiona had
finished a general activity class in the day-room.

Fall foul of your double-crossing boyfriend and you'll
be similarly motivated, thought Fiona, but she only said
mildly, 'Chalk it up to age and experience, Pru. Now is
there anything I can help you with while I've got a
minute?'

Pru said she'd be very glad if Fiona could tell her why
a patient with right-sided sciatica also had numbness on
the outer side of her left foot. By the time they'd sorted
that out, it was time to leave the ward.

As they passed the open door of the doctors' room,
Greg called out, 'Miss Graham!'

'Rather you than me,' whispered Pru. 'He sounds
awful cross.'

Fiona had noticed that, too. She went no further than
the doorway and waited there, stony-faced.

'The next sports injuries meeting is at St Catherine's
College today fortnight.'

'Thank you Mr Monteith. I'll make a note of that.'

'Are you sure you can fit it into your busy social
schedule?'

'Work always takes priority,' Fiona answered crisply,
chin well up.

He didn't look convinced as he asked, 'Have you
heard from the committee of the Olympia Club yet?'

'A letter arrived this morning?'

'And?'

'I am considering the matter.' She hadn't even opened the thing yet, but she meant to keep her options open.

'It's a post for which you are very well qualified.'

So he wanted rid of her, did he? 'I know,' said Fiona grimly. 'Were there any queries arising from the ward round?'

'No—none.'

'So everything is satisfactory from the physio standpoint.'

'You would naturally conclude that,' he supposed.

'Well, either it is or it isn't,' said Fiona belligerently.

'Because everything is either black or white to you.'

'Grey suggests compromise—and I'm not too hot on compromise.'

'Your life must be one long confrontation, then,' he answered. 'Perhaps you should learn a little tolerance.'

'One thing that I will *never* tolerate is deceit!' hissed Fiona, too mad now to know whether that was wise or not.

Greg raised a sceptical eyebrow. 'But only in others, of course,' he returned smoothly. 'You obviously believe your own conduct to be beyond reproach.'

'Pots shouldn't call kettles black,' she retorted haughtily, turning on her heel and flouncing off before she burst into tears.

Until that scene with Greg, Fiona hadn't seriously considered applying for the job at the Olympia Club. Now she found herself wondering if it wasn't heaven-sent. If only it didn't mean leaving Hugh in the lurch. . .

'Your stepfather rang about an hour ago,' reported Hugh as soon as Fiona put her head round the office door. 'I offered to put him through to you, but he said not to bother if you were busy. Then he asked me to tell you——' he looked at the note he'd made '—thanks for your letter and not to worry, it was just one of those things and he thinks he can see how it came about.'

'Was that all? He didn't ask for me to ring him back?'

'No. Apparently he was pressed for time.'

'I see—well, thanks, Hugh.' Fiona thrust aside her personal concerns to ask what sort of day he'd had.

'Boring,' was the verdict. 'I'll be glad when this damned leg allows me to do some real work. How are things on the unit?'

They then discussed Marion's domain until Carol arrived to take her husband home.

Now Fiona could consider her stepfather's reaction to her letter. Clearly, he wasn't as offended by her denial as her mother had been, but was that due to charity or indifference? I don't register enough to arouse his anger, she assumed. But what was new about that?

She opened the letter from the Olympia, and the salary they offered made her gasp. She could buy a car and take foreign holidays, as well as having more time to herself. But time to do what? She'd miss the comradeship of the hospital, the fatigue at the end of the day, but also the feeling of a necessary job well done. And did she really want more time to brood about the mess she seemed to be making of her life?

As well as the offer of a job, there had been a note from Lance in her post that morning—a very polite little note explaining why he couldn't ask her out to dinner before Saturday: an old girlfriend, long-standing, didn't want to hurt her feelings, would be easing her out of his life gradually, hoped she understood.

Yes, Fiona quite understood. It was easy enough to be understanding when you were neither emotionally involved nor even much attracted to a man. Yet even an evening with him would have been preferable to the empty hours yawning ahead. What to do? Something to eat at the wine bar, then home to ring a few old friends and distant cousins. They would all be wondering why she hadn't contacted them before. But Fiona soon discovered that she'd chosen the wrong evening for this. 'Thanks, but it's nothing in particular,' she said the fourth time she was invited to leave a message. 'Unless you could just mention that Fiona called.'

Just Fiona. It would be wonderful to be more than 'just Fiona' to somebody. . .

'And apart from anything else, the wards are half-empty,' exaggerated Fiona as she and Sue sat together over a coffee after their canteen lunch the following Friday.

'Not for long,' said Sue. 'Old Caldwell will be back from convalescent leave soon and Greg is aiming to leave the waiting list about half what he was when he took over.'

'That ought to please the unit manager.'

'That's exactly what I told Greg, and he said—but on second thoughts I'm too much of a lady to tell you what *he* said. You'll just have to use your imagination.' Sue played with the spoon in her saucer. 'How are you finding him these days?'

'The unit manager? I can't say I——'

'No, not the unit manager. Greg.'

'I'm—not sure I know him well enough to pass an opinion.'

Sue let that go by with only the hint of a smile, but persisted, 'You don't think he seems kind of gloomy and preoccupied?'

Fiona refused to be drawn. 'I wouldn't have said either the one or the other.' And that because 'down-right unpleasant' would have been nearer the mark! 'Perhaps he's just a bit depressed about the prospect of demotion when Mr Caldwell comes back.' Clever old me, thinking of that, she told herself.

'What—when they're saying he's almost sure to get the new A and E consultancy at the General?'

'Are they? I didn't know that.' *I wonder how my dear little sister will like having her precious Lambikins permanently on shift work?*

'And you're looking rather shattered yourself these days,' said Sue, coming down off the fence and trying shock tactics.

'Too many late nights,' retorted Fiona with a well-contrived yawn. She waited a second for that hint to take hold before telling Sue how worried she was about the bridegroom, as they always called him. 'That soft-tissue injury on his left foot isn't healing as fast as it should and the amount of mineral water he's drinking makes me wonder if he isn't a diabetic.'

'Well-spotted, that girl,' said Sue, accepting the diversion. 'You're only about a week behind the medics. They're hoping to control it with diet alone, but it's Greg's guess that the medical consultant will prescribe insulin when he comes to see the boy again this afternoon.'

By the time Sue had finished speaking, Fiona had finished her coffee. 'By the way, did I tell you that Marion will be back on Monday?'

'You did—twice. Which suggests to me that you'll be glad to get off my unit. I wonder why?'

'Because I can't be in two places at once and if Marion wasn't back before Moira went on maternity leave I'd have had to attempt it.'

'I thought you were supposed to be Hugh's deputy and chief manipulator of backs and things.'

'On paper, yes. In practice I'm stand-in for any senior who happens to be off. Wards take priority—keep the patients moving in the interests of quick through-put—so the backs either go on a waiting list and get worse or they pay for private treatment elsewhere. And if word then gets round that hospital physios can't treat backs it's not the purse-holders who are left with red faces!'

'My, we are feeling waspish today,' said Sue. 'There's obviously a bug going round—and it's my opinion that you and Greg have both caught it.'

'Then I'd better shove off before I give it to you,' returned Fiona, getting up from the table. 'I'll be helping out in the department until four, and then I'll come up to the unit again to see the day's ops with the juniors. See you then.'

'I can't wait,' Sue responded, giving Fiona the uncomfortable feeling that her friend knew exactly what lay behind her evasiveness. Yes, it was a very good thing that Marion would be back on Monday, though how she would react to the changes Fiona had made remained to be seen.

'So what it comes down to is this,' she was saying to Hugh five minutes later. 'We're now making full use of the unit's little gym and there's a maintenance class daily in every ward, to take care of the exercises common to all, which leaves more time for individual work. And finally the combined case discussion with the nurses during lunch-break on Wednesdays will oblige Marion to smarten up and work more methodically if she's not to be compared unfavourably with her juniors. I'm afraid she'll get a bit of a shock, but with time being so short. . . Besides, who knows when we'd have got another chance?'

'You're a wee wonder—that's what you are,' said Hugh warmly. 'And if you dare to apply for that job at the Olympia Club, I'll write you such a damning reference that they'll withdraw their offer on the spot!'

'When did I tell you that they'd offered me a job?' she demanded.

'You didn't—Greg did.' And she might have guessed that.

'He had no business to do that.'

'Oh, come on! He's my best pal. Besides, he doesn't think it would be right for you.'

'That is not the impression I got when we discussed it.'

'What went wrong, Fiona?' asked Hugh, his voice dropping to a confidential level.

'I don't know what you mean,' she was saying, when they were interrupted, to her great relief.

'That's your first manip ready and waiting, Fiona,' said Sharon.

'Do your exercises and then keep that leg up for half an hour,' Fiona told the boss before dashing off, followed by his knowing chuckle.

'You haven't given the grass much time to grow this afternoon, Fiona,' said Dulcie some time later. 'I make that nine new backs now. How do you propose to fit them in when Moira goes off?'

'That's not before Monday week and if I treat them daily most of 'em should be better by then.'

'And if Marion doesn't come back on Monday after all?'

'I shall start evening sessions. I've been considering that anyway. Too many of our patients have to take time off work.'

'We used to have evening sessions every week until Admin stopped them on account of the cost.'

'What cost?'

'Oh, heating and lighting and overtime for us and the cleaners, who had to come in at funny hours.'

'Yet it's OK for them to work flexi hours to fit in with their golf, I hear. And when you think of all the money that's wasted. . .'

'I'd rather not, if it's all the same to you,' retorted Dulcie. 'I'm ower-young for getting a stroke.'

'Me, too,' laughed Fiona. 'Now it's back to Ortho for

a bit. Have a nice weekend.' I should have realised about the evenings, Fiona thought as she went. A man of Hugh's energy and vision would have had that up and running long since—if allowed. I wonder if he ever wishes he'd stuck to medicine? Probably not. Things aren't exactly rosy for doctors any more—the interference they get. If I had my way, every NHS manager would do six months minimum as an orderly on the wards first. That'd teach 'em at least some of what they don't know or don't believe about caring for the sick and injured!

'You've had a bad afternoon,' diagnosed Angus when he saw Fiona's grim expression.

'Not really—just suffering from a bad attack of the dreaded red tape worm. So what have we got, then?'

'Two hip replacements, an arthrodesis of ankle, a cruciate ligament repair, some sort of new-fangled operation of Mr Monteith's for recurrent dislocation of a shoulder—and that's only his list. The senior reg has been firing on all cylinders too.' Angus pulled a face. 'Somebody really should come in tomorrow morning.'

'Well, don't look at me,' said Fiona. 'I've got enough outpatients coming to keep me going all day. You were on last Saturday, so it'd better be Pru.'

'She won't like it,' warned Angus.

'Tough,' said Fiona.

'The unit administrator is her uncle by marriage.'

'Bu—oh, bother!' substituted Fiona for the preferred expletive. That was a tricky one when, officially, physios were on a five-day week, except for emergencies.

'It's really down to the surgeons for operating on a Friday,' suggested Angus.

'And in due course they'll probably get their knuckles rapped for such devotion to duty,' Fiona returned. 'It's my considered opinion that the hospital world has gone mad.'

'Because surgeons have the temerity to operate on Friday?' Greg asked superciliously from right behind them. He had been able to creep silently up on them because of the new carpet, which nobody liked because chair and trollery wheels went wonky on it.

'Because these days patients are somehow expected to get by without treatment at weekends,' Fiona corrected crisply.

'That is probably the most intelligent observation you have made for some time,' Greg retorted, walking on and leaving both physios speechless, Angus from sheer surprise and Fiona from fury.

She recovered first because subconsciously she had been expecting some such thrust. 'Let's get to work and see if we can improve our image,' she observed with remarkable mildness.

While compiling a list of priorities to start Marion off on Monday, Fiona came across three moderately chesty patients, which gave her an idea. She went along to the doctors' room in search of the senior registrar, spotted not five minutes before.

He wasn't there, but Greg was. Fiona backed off, knocking against the doorpost in her anxiety to escape. 'What do you want?' asked Greg, without looking up from the notes he was making.

'Um, just looking for Mr King. I have a—a proposition to put to him.'

Greg looked up then all right. 'Why? Are three men not enough for you?' he asked bitingly.

For a moment Fiona didn't grasp his meaning, then she flushed with vexation. 'That was quite uncalled for,' she retorted angrily. 'You know very well I only wanted to discuss a problem—about treatment.'

'He's down in Casualty,' said Greg, scowling at her, 'so I'm afraid you'll have to make do with me.'

Fiona scowled back. 'All right, then—some of today's operation cases ought to be treated tomorrow.'

'True, but how are you going to manage that—unless they all have cardiac arrests and get transferred to ICU? You know the rules, idiotic though they are.'

'Chests,' retorted Fiona. 'You know how touchy they are on *that* subject since all the stramash about old folk developing hypostatic pneumonia on Geriatrics when weekend cover was withdrawn. Three of our older patients are fairly productive. If a senior doctor said they were at risk, they'd have to have physio. And if, while here, the physio happened to treat a few post-ops—well, who's to know?'

She'd secured both his attention and his agreement now. Unfortunately he chose to let her know that in a very provocative way. 'It's good to know that not all your deviousness has a selfish motive. That is a very good idea. Give me the names and I'll write them up for treatment.'

Fiona's instinct was to flare up and shout, but the office door was wide open, so she controlled it. Choking back her anger, she shut it carefully, before putting her list on the desk in front of him. Then she said, 'It's very unfair of you to keep throwing spiteful remarks at me when our relative positions make it difficult for me to defend myself.'

'Difficult? I'd have said you do it extremely well. You've obviously had a lot of practice.'

'You just can't forgive me for wounding your pride, can you?' she burst out.

'And you just can't forgive me for finding out that you're—less than honest.'

'And you really can't see why I felt it necessary to—to conceal certain facts.'

'No. Why did you?'

'If you need to ask, then you'd never understand!'

'What's that supposed to mean?'

'Think about it!' she exploded. 'Put yourself in my place, if that's not too much trouble. You'll understand all right then.' His blank expression only served to infuriate her further. 'You—you hypocrite!' she breathed furiously before running out and banging the door.

In the changing-room, Fiona found a note hanging on her locker door. 'Your sister rang while you were upstairs,' it said in Sharon's clear, round hand. 'She'll be round about six and she's staying the night.'

'Wonderful,' Fiona told the empty room. 'That is absolutely all I need.'

Deirdre was pacing up and down the pavement outside Brewery Court when Fiona turned the corner. She had a large canvas bag slung over her shoulder. 'You're late,' she accused when Fiona was near enough. 'Hurry up—I want a bath before I go out.'

'If you worked in a hospital, you'd know how impossible it is to predict finishing times,' retorted Fiona as she unlocked the outside door. 'I'm rather surprised that you don't, anyway—with that wonderful doctor boyfriend of yours.'

'I need to talk to you about him,' returned Deirdre, heading for the lift.

Several other people were taking it too, so confidential chat was postponed, but as soon as they were in the flat with the door shut Fiona invited her sister grimly to fire away. She was assuming the worst and wanted to get it over.

But Deirdre went straight to the bathroom and turned on the taps. 'Bath-towel, please, Fiona.'

'In the cupboard at the end of the bath. Deirdre——'

'Have you got any bath oil? My skin gets so dry. . .'

'No, I have not. You said you wanted to talk about—your boyfriend.'

'So I do.' But Deirdre waited until she was nicely settled in a brimming bath that meant there would be no hot water left for her sister. Then she said, 'He's nice—really nice. Quite the nicest boyfriend I've ever had.'

Fiona's spirits sank to zero. *She's going to tell me that they're engaged!*

'The thing is. . . I'm only nineteen and I'm not ready to settle down yet.'

'You're not ready to settle down yet,' Fiona echoed faintly. *He'd actually proposed, then. . .*

'No, I am not. So when Doug Fraser asked me to this party tonight I told him I'd love to go. He's such fun, Fiona—and *what* a voice! He's entering for the next Cardiff Singer of the World competition, and——'

'Presumably you met him at college,' said Fiona, her spirits popping up a notch at the news of Deirdre's latest man.

'Where else? The thing is, Mum would go spare if she knew what I was planning, so I told her I was coming to see you this evening and would be staying the night. So if she asks I was with you all the time. Got it?'

'You want an alibi,' summarised Fiona.

'Are you not the bright one?' asked Deirdre, reaching out for Fiona's sponge. 'You don't mind, do you?' she assumed airily.

Fiona didn't even hear that. Just as she'd hoped, Deirdre was tiring of Greg. What a pity she hadn't done it sooner. Now it was too late. . .

'I expect I'll be very late,' Deirdre announced when she was finally dressed and ready to go. 'So you'd better give me keys.'

'I might be late myself,' returned Fiona, irritated by her sister's calm assumption that she didn't have anything to do that night. 'So what will you tell Mum if she rings to check on you and gets no reply?'

'I'll say we went to a film or something. It doesn't matter what we say as long as we both tell the same story.'

Fiona was struck by a new thought. 'Why is it Mum you're so keen to deceive? Why not the—the boyfriend?' She couldn't say 'Greg'. His name was sticking in her throat.

'Because Mum's afraid that I'll lose him if I amuse myself on the nights he's on call. But why should I be dull, just because he's working? Anyway, Peter trusts me——'

'*Peter*? Who's Peter?' asked Fiona, dazed. Deirdre's casual introduction of a third admirer was very confusing.

'My doctor, of course. Who else? Now do give me keys, please, Fee—I couldn't bear to be late.'

Fiona went to a drawer for her spare keys, but she held on to them while she said, 'Let me get this straight. Your current boyfriend—this doctor Mum's so enchanted with—is called Peter?'

'That's right. Who did you think he was?'

'Greg Monteith.'

'*What*?' Deirdre went off into elaborate giggles. 'Honestly, you are a clown, Fee! He's nice-looking and amusing and all that, but he's so *old*!'

'So what, how. . .why?'

'God, you're nosy! All right—I met him at a party and we got talking and then he took me home. Then I asked him to a college do because horrible, horrible Joel had just gone off and Greg was the most presentable man I knew just then. Then he took me to a perfectly terrible play by some old Russian or Czech or somebody—as a kind of thank-you, I guess—and that was that, as far as I was concerned, though of course *he* wanted to carry on.'

Again those giggles. 'Imagine you thinking I was over the moon about *him*!'

'And Peter?'

'Oh, for heaven's sake!' Deirdre lunged for the keys, but Fiona held them well away. 'Oh, all right! I met Dr Peter Lamb when I went to the health centre to see our family quack about my nerves. He's terribly sweet and he's got this wonderful red sports car, but, as I told you, I'm not ready to settle down yet.' Another lunge, and this time she wrested the keys from her sister. 'Don't wait up,' she directed, rushing out and slamming the door.

As though sleepwalking, Fiona stumbled over to the sideboard and poured herself a large sherry. The clues had all been there, if only she'd been clear-headed and confident enough to spot them. When she'd told her mother that Deirdre's boyfriend had been at the sports club, her mother had mentioned the name Peter, but she'd assumed that her mother meant the persistent young lawyer.

And then Deirdre calling him Lambikins. That was just the sort of daft handle she would dream up for an eager youngster called Peter Lamb. But surely not even she would stick such a fatuous label on a man like Greg!

Greg. Instinct had told her he wasn't the sort of man to play the tawdry game of which she'd suspected him. But when had she ever trusted either her instinct or her judgement? She'd always needed concrete evidence before she could believe anything to her own advantage.

She had felt the attraction between herself and Greg—and been afraid to believe. That attraction might have developed or it might have faded as they got to know one another. By her folly, she'd ensured that they would never have a chance to find out. Fiona couldn't bear to contemplate what she had possibly thrown away.

# CHAPTER NINE

'NICE weekend, Fiona?' asked Hugh briskly when he limped into the office on his elbow crutches on Monday morning.

'Yes—super, thanks. Dinner at that new waterside bistro on Saturday and the RSO concert last night—' She stopped short. Giving Greg's greatest friend the details of her apparently thriving social life wasn't the best way to persuade them that she wasn't as bad as they thought. Don't be silly, Fiona, she chided herself. Men don't tell one another things the way women do. 'The waiting-room is full already, so I'd better get started—unless there's something. . .'

'Not just now, but if you come across any cases you think I could manage. . .' Hugh sounded quite wistful.

'I'll pass them on,' she promised, while knowing how unlikely that was.

'And would you please ask Marion to come and see me before she goes to the wards?' Hugh asked just as Marion herself tapped on the door and looked in.

Fiona left them to it. 'How are you today, Mr Braid?' she asked her first patient.

'Easier, lass, easier. But there's a bit to go yet, I'm thinking.'

'You've only been twice, so I'd be surprised if there wasn't.' Fiona tested his neck movements and palpated the spots that had been tender on his first visit. 'Right! Up on the couch now. I'm going to be a bit more vigorous with you today.'

After him, Fiona treated several backs, her own personal hand-collection, as she called them, and then a self-diagnosing paediatrician with whose diagnosis of 'back strain' she didn't altogether agree. Sometimes low back pain in middle-aged women had a gynaecological cause, when there was no history either of injury or heavy lifting.

'Fiona, could you come, please?' begged Sharon. 'There's a new patient in the waiting-room with a poodle. She refuses to leave it in her car in case it gets stolen and it's already lifted its leg twice. . .'

Fiona excused herself to Dr Lindsay and went to investigate. Politely she pointed out the impossibility of having animals in a place where patients often came with open wounds.

'This *animal*, as you call him, is my child!' declared the woman.

'Then it's a pity you haven't got your child potty-trained,' commented Fiona. 'No dog or no treatment. We really cannot compromise on this.'

She was afraid it was an impasse until the dog obligingly resolved the problem by slipping its collar and haring off towards Casualty, where doctors with more clout than a mere physiotherapist could be relied on to deal with both dog and its frantic owner, now in hot pursuit.

Fiona left Sharon planning a large notice about the non-admission of pets and returned to her patient. Dr Lindsay wanted to know what all the commotion had been about and when Fiona explained she nodded sagely. 'Obviously a childless woman with a transference problem,' she assumed.

'Do you have children?' asked Fiona for her own reasons.

'I've got three, Fiona, and, believe me, they're not an unmixed blessing. I've got a prolapse that needs attention, but while we're one consultant short I can't find time to get it repaired.'

'I wonder if that could be contributing to your backache?' Fiona suggested artfully.

'Well, now that you mention it. . .' owned Dr Lindsay thoughtfully.

Fiona had been thinking of getting Hugh's help with this one. Now she needn't trouble him. Just as well. He had worse to worry about, as she discovered shortly afterwards.

'I've just had Marion in here in floods of tears,' he said when Fiona joined him in the office for a quick sandwich at lunchtime.

'Her mother,' supposed Fiona.

'No, dear—you! She regards the reorganisation as criticism and, since in a way it was, I found that hard to refute. Rather weakly, I said that you and I had jointly decided it was the only way of getting through the work during her absence, and the holidays which are looming.'

'I'd call that clever, not weak,' said Fiona admiringly.

'Thank you. She also accused you of belittling her to Greg, because when she complained to him about interference he told her that he thought your way was a vast improvement.'

'Oh, poor Marion!' Fiona's sympathy was genuine, but she was also cheered by Greg's approval, however restricted.

So when Greg himself appeared a few minutes later she risked a tentative smile. He met that with a blank stare and said to Hugh, 'We're going to have to do something about Marion Brown. I can't have her going round the place weeping and red-eyed and confiding her troubles to the patients. Besides, she's done damn all in the way of work this morning.'

'I'll come back later,' muttered Fiona, slipping out quietly.

Now what to do? Going to the staffroom would only

make a bad situation worse if Marion was there. Fiona hung about in the main treatment-room until she heard Greg's firm steps receding down the corridor. Then she rejoined Hugh.

He was on the phone, but he beckoned her in and pointed to a chair. 'Great!' he exclaimed soon after. 'You're a gem, Tom, and I think Miss Brown will be grateful too. That's if she doesn't accuse *me* of interference,' he added as he replaced the phone.

'You're safe from criticism,' guessed Fiona confidently. 'You're a *man*.'

Hugh grinned briefly before saying, 'Greg thinks that Marion is heading for a nervous breakdown, and I agree. The poor girl has had too much on her plate for far too long. That was Tom Baird, one of the geriatricians I was talking to, and he's agreed to do a domiciliary visit to old Mrs Brown. Would you believe she's never been assessed? Some mix-up when one GP trainee left and another took over.'

'So if her mother is admitted for assessment and Marion gets a decent rest. . .'

'All may yet be well.'

'What Marion really needs, though, is to get right away for a proper holiday,' said Fiona. 'Moira was telling me she hasn't managed that for years. Do you think you'll manage to persuade her?'

'I'll have a damn good try—and in any case I've promised Greg to take her off his unit until she's in a more stable state.'

'How the blazes will we manage, Hugh? Moria goes on maternity leave after the end of this week.'

'So does the junior assistant personnel manager, but she's important enough to get locum cover. What wouldn't I give for just one minute——? No, I mustn't go down that road, or I'll end up in just as bad a state as poor Marion! Now then, let's imagine the worst possible

scenario, with two of our seniors off on extended leave
and a third not volunteering to cancel his holiday—as
he's a perfect right to do.'

They discussed ways and means and no way could
they contrive even skeleton cover, unless Hugh took an
active share.

'But you can't!' exclaimed Fiona in horror when he
suggested that. 'Too much full-weight-bearing and——'

'With a bit of luck, my bloody femur will come
unstuck, I'll sell the horror story to the tabloids and
there'll be questions asked in the House!' he said
savagely. Fiona had never seen him so angry. 'Carol
wants me to chuck hospital work and start a private
practice. Care to come in with me?'

She knew he didn't mean it, so she said, 'You forget—
I'm being head-hunted by the smartest sports club in
town.'

'So you are—and you'd be mad not to go for it. No,
forget I said that,' he ordered immediately. 'And now
you'd better hotfoot it up to Ortho before Marion does.
I haven't told her she's off that unit yet.'

'Then I'll ask her to come and see you.'

Hugh said, thanks that was very brave of Fiona, when
Marion had taken such a dislike to her.

Fiona couldn't remember another afternoon like it.
Half an hour in the wards, half an hour back in the
department to see patients nobody else could treat,
giving Sharon the awful job of cramming as many of her
OPs as possible into the afternoon, as she would be
doubling duties for the foreseeable future.

'If I did this without asking, you'd give me hell,'
muttered Sharon.

'I know, but this is an emergency.'

'When is it not, in this department?' asked Sharon.
'There's more shuffling goes on here than—than in
a casino!'

Inevitably, all that dodging back and forth meant that Fiona was running very late and an enforced break for patients' high tea meant more delay.

'I was just goin' to take oot ma teeth and try for a nap,' said her last patient, somewhere around half-seven.

'I wouldn't say no to a nap myself,' returned Fiona, stifling a yawn.

'Aye, ye look as though you could do with one,' agreed the man. 'So what are you going to do with yon wee radio, hen?'

'It's not a radio, Mr Tennant, it's for reducing the swelling round your foot.' Normally, she'd put some ice on it first, but it had been so long in the canister today that it had gone all mushy.

'And is that supposed to work?' asked the man when Fiona had finished. 'I didn't feel a thing.'

'Not all physiotherapy hurts,' Fiona told him with a tired smile. 'A day or two of this treatment and the foot will feel much softer and pliable.' That was a rotten explanation. Good thing he's my last. . .

'Just so long as it doesnae melt ma bones.'

'It'll certainly not do that.' A full-scale yawn this time.

'Yes, you're certainly needin' a nap,' he decided, eyes gleaming. 'I'll just move over and ye can bunk up wi' me.'

Fiona thanked him kindly, but said she couldn't risk hurting his bad foot, and anyway she was going off duty now.

It was too late and far too much trouble to cook supper, so Fiona went across the road to the wine bar. The evening rush was at its height and she had difficulty in finding a seat. Only after she'd sat down did she realise that she was just across the gangway from Greg and his pretty house officer.

He merely nodded, but the girl asked sympathetically, 'Is this you only just finished work, then, Fiona?'

Fiona nodded, decided that was inadequate in the face of the girl's friendliness and told her, 'We're going through a bit of a staff crisis at the moment, what with the boss's accident and so on.' She'd probably heard about Marion, too.

'Yes, that accident was the most awful luck. How's he doing?'

'As well as can be expected—provided he doesn't do anything reckless,' said Greg before Fiona could reply.

'That's very informative,' laughed the girl, apparently unaware of the constraint between her two companions. So much unaware, in fact, that when the couple at their table left she invited Fiona to join them.

It seemed less embarrassing all round to accept. But five minutes later, when the waitress brought Greg a bowl of soup, Dr Cox thanked him for her coffee, looked at her watch and said she'd better dash before the library shut or she wouldn't get those books he'd recommended.

'Oh, dear!' exclaimed Fiona. 'That is, I thought you were together.'

'So we were, in a manner of speaking, but Mary got here first.'

'Anyway, I'm sorry. Would you like me to move?'

'Where to?' he asked. Her place across the aisle had been taken and there wasn't another vacant chair in sight.

'I just thought. . .'

'I wouldn't if I were you,' he advised. 'Your thought processes have been seriously out of order of late.'

'And rather illogical as well,' she added; a tentative first step towards admitting she'd been wrong—something she'd been longing to do ever since that enlightening talk with Deirdre.

Greg's gloom didn't lighten. 'Logical thought is rather rare in your sex,' he stated.

'I don't agree!'

'Naturally—you're a woman.'

'Thank you for pointing that out—I hadn't realised.'

'Now you're being silly,' he told her, preparing to leave.

'What about your supper?' she asked, wanting to detain him.

'I've had all I've got time for. I'm on stand-by for A and E tonight. Yours is not the only department under pressure.'

Fiona looked down and away. This was the end, then. She'd made a gesture—no matter how small—but he would have seized it had he wanted to. He hadn't needed any encouragement at all in the beginning. But then in the beginning he hadn't known what a mixed-up and peculiar person she was. When you really got down to it, there wasn't much to choose between her and Marion!

The next few days were hectic, to say the least—starting at eight, seeing two or three manipulation cases who couldn't come in the afternoons, haring off to Orthopaedics, then back to Physio for a brief lunch-break. Four solid hours of outpatients next, then back to Ortho to treat those patients she hadn't got around to in the morning. If she got home by half-seven, Fiona felt that she'd done amazingly well.

'You're quite mad,' was Sue's assessment of that timetable.

Lance said the same thing, but more forcibly, when she rang his office at lunchtime on Friday to tell him she couldn't go out with him that night. 'I didn't have you down for a wimp, Fiona. I frequently work a sixteen-hour day.'

'Yes, but sitting on your backside with a computer, a telephone and a PA to fetch and carry,' she hit back. 'Physiotherapy is heavy manual work, I'll have you know.'

'I'm not used to being stood up,' he snarled.

'And I'm not used to being called a wimp!'

'Will I see you again?' he asked.

'Maybe—if the NHS ever gets its act together.'

'One down and two to go,' assumed Hugh as Fiona banged down the phone.

'What are you talking about?' asked Fiona, mystified.

'I was referring to your gentleman friends.'

'I don't remember discussing them with you. . .'

'One hears things,' explained Hugh.

'Then I can only say that reports of my love life are greatly exaggerated,' Fiona retorted. 'In fact, it's non-existent, if you really want to know.' Now go and tell that to your best friend—*please*, dear Hugh!

'If that's true, then I'd say it was your own fault,' he said, not too sympathetically.

'I prefer to think I was born under an unlucky star—it's more romantic.' Fiona bit into the stale sandwich she hadn't had time to eat the day before. 'By the way, did you know that Marion hasn't gone away after all? Sister Robertson saw her in the car park last night.'

Hugh frowned. 'That's odd. Marion told me she'd booked into an hotel at Pitlochry.'

'Sue actually spoke to her, and Marion said she'd just been visiting her mother.'

'Some folk just will not be helped,' said Hugh, reaching for the phone.

'What are you going to do?' asked Fiona.

'Ring her and tell her that she has a duty to her patients and her colleagues, as well as to her mother. She's on sick leave, with orders from her GP to get right away.'

'Then I hope she takes more notice of you than you do of me when I tell you to take care of that leg,' reproved Fiona, leaving her coffee and darting out before he could throw something.

When Fiona returned to Orthopaedics later on that afternoon, the senior registrar was looking out for her. She had walked on to the unit wincing, with her right hand clasped to her left shoulder, which she was carefully circling through a full range of movement.

'Practising to join a cricket team?' he asked jocularly.

'Hoping I haven't given myself a rotator cuff lesion,' she explained. 'I suppose you've got a job for me. . . Hey, you—stand still!' she roared at a man spotted hirpling down the corridor in a long leg plaster and without crutches. ''Scuse me,' she said to the startled registrar as she ran for a wheelchair and parked the patient in it. 'Walk without crutches again and I'll flatten you,' she told him. 'He'll need a check X-ray, will he not?' she asked the registrar.

He confirmed that and added his own reproof to Fiona's. By then, they'd both forgotten why he wanted to speak to her.

Fiona found that several patients objected to being treated so late in the day, when visiting was imminent. Mrs Mercer, for instance. 'You can leave me, hen. I'll do my exercises myself when I've got a minute.'

'But you can't, my dear. You need my help.'

'Call that help?' she puffed when Fiona had urged her to try and bend her knee and then stretch it against strong resistance. 'Seems more like hindrance to me.'

Fiona explained the purpose of it all. 'You could say it's a bit like trying to shift a rusty bolt.'

'For mercy's sake—I'd just take a few drops of Three in One to that.'

'And strong static muscle work like this increases the joint's own natural lubrication, so you're not far out.'

'You'd talk your way into heaven, lassie,' declared Mrs Mercer.

But not back into Greg's good books. Not that I've really tried. . . Fiona walked slowly towards the exit, thinking about that. The door of the doctors' room stood open and a discreet glance in passing showed her Greg in there alone, reading X-rays.

'Ahem—excuse me,' said Fiona from the open doorway. 'I just wondered if Hugh had told you we're starting a waiting list for outpatient treatment.' As openers went, that was pretty feeble, but she was desperate.

'Yes, thank you—he has.' And as a response that was less than encouraging.

'Of course, if there were patients who were desperately urgent, I could probably——'

'When?' he asked baldly.

Their eyes met and held, expressionless, hiding their emotions.

'I hate this!' she burst out, starting towards him.

'So do I,' he responded with a heavy sigh.

'Then *surely*. . .!'

'Be realistic,' he said heavily. 'Workloads increase and staff levels go down. And there's damn all we can do about it. Have you finished? Work—for the day,' he added when she just stood there, frozen in disappointment.

Fiona pulled herself together. 'Not quite—just a few outpatients I'm hoping to be able to discharge before the—the ban. . .'

'You'll end up like Marion,' he warned, which was about the most depressing thing he could possibly have said.

'I wouldn't be at all surprised,' breathed Fiona bitterly, turning away quickly before he saw the tears of frustration welling up and stinging her eyelids.

When she had burst out like that about hate, she'd been referring to the depths to which their once promising relationship had sunk. But Greg had thought she meant their working conditions because, these days, he only thought of her in the context of work. Only a miracle could reverse the situation now—and Fiona didn't believe in miracles.

It was such a beautiful evening. When Fiona finally emerged into the evening sunlight for the short walk home, the air was warm on her bare arms. Would this wonderful weather last until things quietened down enough for her to take a holiday?

As she crossed the car park, she met Greg, taking the long way round from Ortho to A and E. 'I thought I may as well see as much of the sun as possible,' he explained. 'Fiona——' She waited, breathless, wondering what was coming. 'If you find that you're too busy to come to the next sports injuries session, Hugh will come. He can easily deliver his spiel sitting down.'

And is that Hugh's idea—or yours? she wondered with a stab of disappointment. 'Whatever you both decide,' she agreed quietly. 'As for me, I'm past caring one way or the other.'

'Yes, you're having a rotten time,' he acknowledged in a gentler tone.

'I'll survive,' she supposed.

'Life is about rather more than mere survival.'

'I've heard that before somewhere,' she responded, a tiny spark of hope flaring within her.

If only the duty casualty officer hadn't come to the entrance just then and called out to Greg, who knew what he might not have gone on to say? But he'd been summoned and had to run to answer the call.

Reluctantly, Fiona continued on her way to the gate,

lost in thought. Perhaps if next time we meet I were to say this—or do that. . .

She started violently when Marion stepped out from behind a parked van, right in her path, and she said the first thing that came into her head. 'You're supposed to be miles away on holiday, Marion!'

Marion's eyes were wild. 'You'd like that, wouldn't you?' she snarled. 'Get poor old Marion out of the way and it's all mine! But I'm not like you. I *care* about others! I've just been visiting my mother,' she added quite mildly, in marked contrast to the venomous tone she'd used before.

'That's very creditable, but you ought to think of yourself too, you know. Hugh thinks——'

'Hugh thinks exactly what you tell him to think nowadays!' hissed Marion. 'He never gave me anything but praise until *you* turned up! You've got them all on a string, have you not? With your smiles and your so-called expertise and your big brown eyes! Hugh, Greg. . .' Her voice gave out on a sob.

'Stop it, Marion!' Fiona rapped out. 'Calm down,' she went on more quietly. 'You're overwrought—don't know what you're saying. I'm on your side—we all are.'

'You're not—sneaking in behind my back and turning them all against me. *I'm* Greg's physio—*I* should be helping him with those talks. I could do it—I could do anything he asked of me. Make him happy, look after him——' She seized Fiona's shoulders and shook her violently. 'Why did you have to come here? I hate you! It's all your fault. . .' She let go of Fiona and began to cry, huge noisy sobs which racked her body and threatened to choke her.

Fiona was both frightened and horrified, but she was also full of pity. She laid a trembling hand on Marion's arm, willing the right words to come. 'Marion, listen——'

But Marion jerked free with a snarl of rage. Then with both hands she gave Fiona a mighty shove that threw her backwards to the ground. And on the way down Fiona struck her head on a sharp corner of the van.

Because she was shocked and half stunned, it was several seconds before Fiona could sit up. Warm blood was pouring down her neck and soaking her blouse from a deep cut on her scalp. She felt sick and shaken and her limbs were smarting from contact with the rough ground. Eventually she managed to struggle into a sitting position, but when she looked round fearfully Marion had gone.

Fiona forced herself to think constructively. She couldn't possibly walk home in this state and neither could she seek help in Casualty—there would be too many awkward questions asked. She must go back to Physio, clean herself up and then ring for a taxi. Shakily she got to her feet and went stumbling back the way she'd come.

She was stopped by the Casualty porter, who was pushing an empty chair. 'I was on the way to pick up a patient from X-ray,' he said, 'but I reckon he can wait. In you get, m'lass.'

'No—thanks. I'll be all right.'

'Good God, it's you, Miss Graham,' he realised with shock. 'I didn't recognise you in that state.' He ignored her protests and thrust her into the chair, asking, 'What in glory happened, hen? Were ye knocked down? The polis——'

'No, nothing like that,' she insisted, appalled at the idea of the police getting involved. 'I just—fell.'

'Is that so?' She could tell he didn't believe her. 'Och, well, they'll soon have ye sorted. Lucky you weren't too far away.'

They were heading fast for Casualty and Fiona said,

No, not there—she'd been on her way to Physio. 'Things to do. . .'

'Sorry, lass,' said her rescuer firmly, 'but this is one time when it's staff before patients. You cannae see it, but you've a gey great gash on your head that needs stitching, if I'm any judge.'

All the cubicles were full and there were several patients waiting, so after a whispered word with the receptionist the porter wheeled Fiona into the doctors' room. 'They'll soon have ye sorted,' he repeated, before going off to find a doctor.

Fiona still hadn't decided on her story, when the door opened to admit the young casualty officer who had hailed Greg not long before. 'Hello, Miss Graham,' he said. 'Bob says you were knocked down. A car, was it?'

'No, I fell. I sort of tripped—and fell.'

He was already inspecting her head wound. 'What— backwards? That's unusual,' he returned, immediately highlighting the weakness of her explanation.

'Then perhaps—yes, I think it was. The ground was slippery,' Fiona answered desperately. 'I don't exactly remember. I'm feeling rather faint.'

'I'll bet. This is one hell of a gash you've got here. I think we'd better get you X-rayed, once we've tidied you up.'

'No, surely. . .'

'Dinnae ye be teaching yer grannie tae suck eggs, lassie,' he ordered with a grin. 'We have to take care of our physios. I was hearing that you're falling by the wayside like skittles. Is there anybody you'd like to phone? Bob said you were on your way to work.'

'Not patients—just a few reports. . .' A sudden wave of nausea and faintness engulfed her and she swayed in the chair. At once he wheeled her out of the room, found a free cubicle and settled her comfortably on the examination couch. Then he sent an orderly for a glass of water, which Fiona drank gratefully.

Lying there, eyes closed, she gradually realised that the low-voiced conversation on the other side of the drawn curtain was about herself. '. . . and a large scalp wound in the right occipito-temporal region. She says she thinks the ground was slippery, but I'd be more inclined to believe that in January than June. It's my belief that she was attacked—and pretty nastily at that.'

'Let's get her fixed up and worry about details afterwards,' she heard Greg answer urgently before he swished back the curtain to gaze down on her in horror and concern. 'Fiona—my dear girl. . .' The anxiety in his voice was all that was needed to unlock the tears she'd been holding back.

She held out a shaking hand. 'Oh, Greg. . .' He came close and took her hand. Then, with a smothered groan, he put his free arm round her shoulders. 'There, there, honey—that's right, let it out. . .'

She turned her face into his shoulder, taking comfort from his nearness. When she'd calmed down a bit, he said gently, 'We need to fix you up, Fiona.'

'I know—and I'm sorry to be so silly.'

'That all depends on what you're referring to,' he murmured as his fingers gently and skilfully explored her wound. 'Some of this lovely hair will have to come off. . .'

'I expected that.'

'How did you get this?'

'I fell,' she insisted quickly.

He left it at that and picked up an opthalmascope to examine her eyes for signs of brain damage. 'Seems all right,' he murmured then. 'Now think carefully—this is very important. Were you knocked out when you—fell? Even for seconds?'

'No, I don't think so. I was dazed for a minute—still am, come to that—but I knew where I was, and so on.'

'Good. Now listen, dear. We're going to stitch this wound and deal with the hundred and one abrasions you also seem to have collected; then we're going to X-ray your skull, though I don't expect it to show anything.'

'Anything you say, Greg,' she whispered.

'Careful, or I'll be sure you're concussed,' he whispered before straightening up and calling his colleague. 'Fiona lives alone,' he explained, 'so she can't possibly go home in this state. Find her a bed for the night, will you?'

That was when Fiona passed out.

'And how do you feel this morning?' asked a bright young voice close to Fiona's right ear about two minutes after she awoke next morning.

Fiona opened her eyes wide with surprise and stared all round the tiny room. Then it all came back. 'Like I've been trampled on by a herd of elephants,' she confessed, carefully shifting her aching limbs.

'What about your head, though?'

'Throbbing like mad, but it's definitely still there.'

The nurse laughed. 'You'll do,' she said. 'Could you eat breakfast?'

'Couldn't I just—I'm starving!' Fiona remembered having eaten nothing since lunch the previous day.

'That sounds encouraging. Back in a minute, then.'

Fiona heaved herself up in the bed and looked round. Surgical Neurology, she guessed from the décor. Her clothes lay neatly folded on a chair—all except her blouse, which some thoughtful soul had washed and draped over the radiator. It would have been spattered with blood, she supposed.

When the nurse returned with a breakfast of boiled egg, cereal and toast—'Well, you did say you were starving!'—she also told Fiona that she could go home as soon as the registrar had given her the all-clear.

Fiona was up and dressed by the time he came. She was also ready with a plausible version of her accident, but he didn't question her about that, just handed her enough pain-killers for the weekend and told her to take more water with it next time. Then he told her to report back to the unit on Monday morning for a final check.

They had thoughtfully ordered a taxi for her, and she'd arrived home and paid it off before remembering that she'd told several of her outpatients to come for treatment that morning. Once in the flat, she went straight to phone in her apologies, but before she could do so the doorbell rang.

She was surprised to see Greg standing on the mat. He was dressed casually in light trousers and a cheerful patterned shirt. She remembered it was his weekend off. She also remembered the foolish way she'd behaved the night before. 'Er, hello,' she said awkwardly. 'I was just going round the corner. Some outpatients coming. . .'

He took her gently but firmly aside, came in and shut the door. 'Hugh's right about you,' he said. 'You're not just conscientious, you're obsessional. I phoned him last night to tell him about the attack on you and he's dealing with all outstanding problems.'

The passage was narrow and they were too close for sensible thought. Attack, he'd said. Attack. . . Fiona led the way to the living-room, where she turned to face him. 'I didn't say I was attacked.'

'You didn't need to—your injuries told the tale. And the fact that you keep denying it suggests that you know your attacker. So who was it, Fiona?'

She should have realised he was only here to get at the truth, when all accidents on hospital property must be fully documented. How stupid, then, to feel so disappointed!

'Who was it, Fiona?' Greg repeated.

She steadied herself by grasping the back of the chair she'd unconsciously put between them. 'First, I need to know that this will go no further. I absolutely refuse to get—anybody into trouble.'

'It was Marion, wasn't it?' he asked then.

'Why should you think that?'

'Because I met her in the grounds last night, not long before I met you. She was edgy and upset and I was— less sympathetic than I might have been. I told her she was helping nobody by disobeying orders. She started to cry and I told her to pull herself together. I think she saw us meet and talk—and waited for you.'

'All right—yes, it was Marion. But I'll deny it if there's a fuss.'

'There needn't be a fuss, but as she's obviously far more seriously disturbed than any of us realised, then for her own sake her doctor must be told.'

'Why? She sees me as the cause of all her troubles, so she's not likely to bash anybody else.'

'If the situation were reversed, would you assault Marion?'

'No, of course not. Though I'd probably feel like it.'

'Point proved,' he said. 'Now let's forget about her for a bit. How are *you* feeling this morning?'

'Much better, thank you. Quite all right, in fact. But thank you very much for asking. Why are you looking at me like that?'

He came closer, looking at her harder than ever. 'Back to square one again,' he sighed. 'So what's your excuse this time?'

'I don't think I know what you mean. . .'

He threw his arms out sideways and clenched his fists. 'Much more of this and you'll be in danger of provoking another assault! Even at your best, you were never very encouraging. And your confounded pride took such a knock when I found out you'd been at such pains to hide your family connections—though heaven only knows why you thought that was necessary. . . So, when you made it clear that you wanted nothing more to do with me, I accepted it. I have my pride, too, and I'm not the kind of man to go on battering his head against a brick wall for too long. Then last night you seemed so—so happy to see me that I. . . Clearly I was wrong. I shouldn't have come here. I'm sorry!'

He was halfway to the door before Fiona managed to call out his name. He came back and paused in the doorway, eyeing her warily.

'It was all a dreadful mistake,' she faltered.

Hope died in his eyes as he said coldly, 'So it would seem.'

'Oh, God, why can I never say the right thing to you?' she cried out. 'I meant *my* mistake—about you and my sister. I found out you were dating her that very first day, when you called for her at the house, but I never knew you'd stopped. Any time I phoned home, she and mother went on and on about her wonderful doctor boyfriend and I thought they meant you. I thought you were seeing us both. At the same time. Or, rather, alternately. That is——'

'Thank you, but I've got the picture,' he said tightly. 'Now just one question. Why the hell didn't you check? Presumably the man has a name. Why didn't you ask what it was?'

'You make it sound so simple,' she breathed.

'It *is* simple! And only a mixed-up idiot with an outsize inferiority complex like yours could possibly think otherwise! How *could* you be so dense, Fiona?'

'That's quite easy when you don't have a lot of self-esteem,' she whispered. 'Though most of the time I function quite well. Really, it's only when I'm up against Deirdre that I seem to go to bits. She's so attractive and—and everything I'm not. And——'

'Your sister,' said Greg very firmly, 'is a spoiled, self-centred brat who is sorely in need of a damn good spanking.'

'So you weren't hurt when she dumped you, then?'

'Dumped *me*?' He was genuinely astounded. Then enlightenment dawned. 'Yes, of course, she would say that, with an outsize ego like hers. The fact is, I lost count of all the messages she left on my answering machine before she finally gave up. Now I suppose you'll accuse me of telling fairy-stories,' he concluded with a sigh.

'No—because you're not conceited, Greg. Confident, yes—but not exactly conceited.'

'Confident—me?' he breathed. 'Not when I'm around you, I'm not! You make me feel like a—a moonstruck teenager.'

'That's funny,' she said, suddenly feeling a whole lot happier. 'That's exactly the effect you have on me!'

'So what are you going to do about it?'

'I—don't really know. . .'

'Well, I do,' he said, bridging the gap and seizing her in his arms.

'Ouch!' breathed Fiona as her battered body protested.

'You're sore, sweetheart,' Greg said tenderly. 'Never mind—I'll kiss every last bruise better.'

And he proceeded to do just that.

# Temptation

# Lost Loves

## 'Right Man...Wrong time'

All women are haunted by a lost love—a disastrous first romance, a brief affair, a marriage that failed.

A second chance with him...could change everything.

Lost Loves, a powerful, sizzling mini-series from Temptation continues in April 1995 with...

### Even Cowboys Get the Blues
### by Carin Rafferty

MILLS & BOON
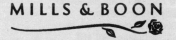

# Paperback Writer...

## Have you got what it takes?

For anyone who has ever thought about writing a **Mills & Boon** Romance, but just wasn't sure where to start, help is at hand...

As a result of ever increasing interest from budding authors, **Mills & Boon** have compiled a cassette and booklet package which explains in detail how to set about writing a romantic novel and answers the most frequently posed questions.

The cassette and booklet contain valuable hints that can be applied to almost any form of creative writing.

There isn't an easy recipe for writing a romance, but our cassette and booklet will help point you in the right direction—just add imagination to create your own success story!

The 40 minute cassette and 28 page booklet are available together in one smart pack from most branches of WH Smith and John Menzies and other leading retailers. Price £9.99.

Or send your cheque (made payable to Harlequin Mills & Boon Ltd) to:
Cassette & Booklet Package, Dept. M.,
P.O. Box 183, Richmond TW9 1ST.

# GET 4 BOOKS AND A MYSTERY GIFT

Return the coupon below and we'll send you 4 Love on Call novels absolutely FREE! We'll even pay the postage and packing for you.

We're making this offer to introduce you to the benefits of Reader Service: FREE home delivery of brand-new Love on Call novels, at least a month before they are available in the shops, FREE gifts and a monthly Newsletter packed with information.

Accepting these FREE books places you under no obligation to buy, you may cancel at any time, even after receiving just your free shipment. Simply complete the coupon below and send it to:

HARLEQUIN MILLS & BOON, **FREEPOST**, PO BOX 70, CROYDON CR9 9EL.

- - - - - - - - - - - - - - - - - - - - - - - - - - - - - - - - - - - - - - - - - -

NO STAMP NEEDED

**Yes,** please send me 4 Love on Call novels and a mystery gift as explained above. Please also reserve a subscription for me. If I decide to subscribe I shall receive 4 superb new titles every month for just £7.20* postage and packing free. I understand that I am under no obligation whatsoever. I may cancel or suspend my subscription at any time simply by writing to you, but the free books and gift will be mine to keep in any case.
*I am over 18 years of age.*

1EP5D

Ms/Mrs/Miss/Mr _____

Address _____

_____

_____

_____ Postcode _____

Offer closes 30th June 1995. The right is reserved to refuse an application and change the terms of this offer. *Prices subject to change without notice. One application per household. Offer not available for current subscribers to this series. Valid in U.K. and Eire only. Overseas readers please write for details. Southern Africa write to: IBS Private Bag X3010, Randburg 2125.

mps MAILING PREFERENCE SERVICE

You may be mailed with offers from other reputable companies as a result of this application. Please tick box if you would prefer not to receive such offers. ☐

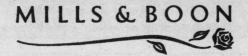

# MILLS & BOON

# LOVE  CALL

## *The books for enjoyment this month are:*

| | |
|---|---|
| **SMOOTH OPERATOR** | Christine Adams |
| **RIVALS FOR A SURGEON** | Drusilla Douglas |
| **A DAUNTING DIVERSION** | Abigail Gordon |
| **AN INDISPENSABLE WOMAN** | Margaret Holt |

---

## *Treats in store!*

Watch next month for the following absorbing stories:

| | |
|---|---|
| **PRACTICE MAKES MARRIAGE** | Marion Lennox |
| **LOVING REMEDY** | Joanna Neil |
| **CRISIS POINT** | Grace Read |
| **A SUBTLE MAGIC** | Meredith Webber |

---

Available from W.H. Smith, John Menzies, Volume One, Forbuoys,
Martins, Tesco, Asda, Safeway and other paperback stockists.

Readers in South Africa - write to:
IBS, Private Bag X3010, Randburg 2125.